COMEUPPANCE DAY

By Louis R Agoston Jr.

A story of revenge, forgiveness and how far a man, seeking redemption, would go for the people he loved.

A fictitious account that many ponder, but few carry out.

CHAPTER 1

Early morning in an abandoned sewage treatment plant, ten people of various backgrounds stood in knee-deep sludge as water rushed in from a twelve inch rusty pipe that was quickly filling the putrid smelling concrete tank. Each of their foreheads bore a number that ranged from 4 to 13 written with a black marker. Some of the captives were still as they stared at the rusty steel grid above them that served as an immovable lid. Others thrashed around desperately in search of an opening. All pleaded for help, for the water was now waist high.

The commotion of the frightened captives and the constant splashing of the inrushing water drowned out the squeaky hinges of the opening door next to the pit. When the thin captor stepped into view and looked down on his victims they shouted at him, but he held up a hand for silence. As they glared at him he began his speech, "I would like to go into detail about how I was able to assemble all of you today; the planning, the hours of preparation, but there is only enough time left to describe the selection process."

Carefully making eye contact with each one he continued, "Over the years, the only things that people remember vividly are the very good things and the very bad things, everything else is just filler. In my life, you were some of the bad things!"

Some of the shorter captives were now frantically treading water or trying to cling to taller ones. The two women, # 10 and # 13 were crying.

"When the police raid my house they will find a list, compiled over the years of 144 people like you who have made my life miserable. Their sins range from ordinary insults to personal injury. Of course, the rankings frequently changed, as some were added, others dropped off."

The cloudy brown sewage water was now high enough that all captives clung onto the rebar screen. As the others looked on, two of the men attempted to remove the locked chain on the only opening from the pit.

Frustrated, one of those men yelled at the captor, "Come on Brian, let me out of here! I said I was sorry."

Brian coldly looked down on the filthy wet man and said, "Yes, Don, I remember."

FLASH BACK #1

In the dimly lit break room at the Janco Metal Fabrication shop, Brian Toth waited for the dreaded meeting with his foreman Don Heiler. Out in the hallway, Brian's friend and co-worker Nathan Kovacs argued with the portly foreman about the pending layoffs.

"Don, he shows up on time every day, does good work and doesn't make any trouble, what do you have against the guy?"

"He's a long haired weirdo. He spends his entire free time running, never says much... just too strange for me."

"You know his situation. He lost his wife this year, but what you may not be aware of is that his son also has the same heart disease that she died from. You'd be wacky too if you had to endure all of that."

"Nate, I have to do what I think is best for the company. It is much cheaper to lay off a couple of guys and have the rest work some overtime to meet production. You ought to be happy that I'm keeping you."

"It's just not right, Don. He really needs this job."

"I'm done talking about it. Get back to work now."

Nathan shook his head and reluctantly retreated to the welding shop. Don watched him leave and then squeezed his obese body through the break room doorway as Brian stood and looked at him with hopeful eyes.

"Well, Brian I hate to do this to you, but work has dropped off a bit, and I'm going to have to let you go."

"Don, I've never asked for any favors from you, but I'll come in for any shift, work weekends and do any job necessary to stay employed."

"It has already been decided, Brian. You can pick up your last check in the office on your way out."

As the foreman turned and walked away from a stunned Brian, he looked back over his shoulder and said in a singsong voice, "Sorry."

With the filthy water up to their shoulders, most of the disgustedly slimy ten begged for forgiveness, but one shrill voice stood out among them. "Brian, give us a chance!"

Brian looked at the pathetic women and could barely make out the number on her forehead, but he would never forget the voice of his high school teacher.

"You are right Margaret, I know you don't believe that everyone deserves a second chance, but I'm going to give you one. So here it is. If any one can tell me how many marathons I have run, I will shut off the water. You can come up with the answer Margaret, just use your head."

The drenched heads looked at each other and hoped that someone would correctly shout out the answer. The only other woman among the bunch stared at Margaret and after coughing out some water, spat and said, "Margaret, he said to 'use your head.' There is a number thirteen on your forehead." Margaret's eyes widened and she blurted out, "Thirteen. You have run thirteen marathons, Brian."

Brian quickly vanished from their sight and in a moment the water ceased filling the pit. When he reappeared, Brian held out a key and dropped it into the slurry. "That was the key to the lock. You can either dive down and retrieve it, or wait an hour for the rescue squad to free you."

Before he headed to his car, Brian added, "Go and sin no more."

CHAPTER 2

Before driving away in his old and dusty blue Chevy Cavalier, Brian opened the trunk and checked the supplies that he had placed there a few days earlier. On the left was a cardboard box that a small microwave oven came in. Brian had altered its appearance with light brown wrapping paper and address stickers to make it look like an official delivery package. He lifted the lid and observed its contents of several lengths of half-inch nylon rope with a roll of duct tape and a black marker. After replacing the top on the box, he rearranged the items on the right side of the trunk. Moving his towel, washcloth and toiletry kit aside, he lifted and inspected his clean clothing. The dark brown uniform consisted of a pair of shorts and a short-sleeved shirt with socks and a baseball cap to match and a pair of black rubber-soled shoes. He sat these items next to a pen and clipboard and carefully unwrapped the oily rag and grasped the large revolver. After inspecting the cylinder of the loaded Ruger .44 Blackhawk, he tucked it away in the trunk and got in the car, started the engine and drove down the gravel road away from the old sewage treatment plant.

Carefully obeying all driving rules, he followed Beaver Creek until it intersected State Route 6 where he turned east and headed toward Bowling Green. As farmland gave way to suburbia, he slowed a bit and marveled at the fine houses on the well-groomed golf course. The two cardiologists who had failed in their attempt to save his wife lived there. Although rather young, they shared the reputation of being the best surgeons in their field. Their specialty was heart transplants. Dr. Richard Bauhner was a playboy who drove sporty cars, liked a lot of attention and thought very highly of himself. He lived in an oversized white brick house near the third green. Dr. Noah Erikson however, was more sensible. He also had a large home, but he shared it with his attractive wife and their five-year-old daughter.

Across from the golf course, a nature preserve left over from the Great Black Swamp, stood in defiance to the ever-expanding subdivisions. Turning into the park, Brian drove past the soccer fields and into the woods and parked at the nature center. He had spent many hours there running laps on the winding tree-covered trails in preparation for his numerous marathons. Today though, he was there to use the facilities to wash up and change into his courier outfit. After taking a sponge bath and shaving, he put on deodorant and dressed. While brushing his teeth and combing his short light brown hair, he nodded approvingly in the mirror at his costume, then exited the building and packed everything into his car. Before closing the trunk, he placed the gun into the box, then picked up the package and clipboard and started walking toward the golf course. Along the way he phoned the authorities.

The female voice of the dispatcher said, "Wood County Sherriff's Department."

"Yes, I'd like to report ten drowning rats at the old Potterville Waste Water Treatment Plant."

"Sir, what is your name and where are you calling from?"

"This call is being recorded isn't it?"

"Yes it is, but we need more information."

"Then listen to the tape and send along many beach towels."

Brian then shut off his cell phone, crossed Wintergarden Road and entered the golf course just before two Wood County Deputies flew by headed west with their flashers on.

CHAPTER 3

When the deputies arrived, they found ten pairs of hands clutching the steel screen over the filthy wastewater. The captives, immersed up to their necks, were very still trying not to make any waves. The first officer said, "Remain calm folks, we'll have you all out in a couple of minutes."

The second officer noticed a bolt cutter conveniently leaning against the pump house building, seized it and cut the lock off. He unwound the chain and lifted the hinged gate, carefully allowing it to come to rest on the metal lattice without pinching anyone's fingers. All of the occupants were subdued except for Don who continued to curse Brian as both deputies pulled him from the slop. While the remaining victims were lifted to freedom, two rescue squads arrived, followed closely by the Channel 12 News van.

The recent graduate of Bowling Green State University was thrilled to be on her first solo live broadcast. Overhearing the dispatcher through the police radio monitor, she had convinced station manager Ben Walters that she knew the exact location of the crime, having grown up in nearby Grand Rapids. Before she could finish reminiscing about how, back in the day, some local teenage boys found it to be an excellent place to park and make out with their girlfriends, her boss took a chance and sent the petite blonde on the assignment.

Quickly exiting the van, Bob the cameraman, began filming the last human extractions. One by one, they were hosed down by the paramedics with clean cold water and then wrapped in blankets. Since Don was the only complainer, he was the first to be placed in a warm vehicle. With the source of the obscenities gone, the stylish young newswoman began her report.

"This is Ashley Ludwig with a live report from the Potterville Waste Water Treatment Plant where ten citizens were just rescued from a sewage container. The details are sketchy at this time, but apparently a local man somehow rounded up these people and darned near drowned them with yucky water in that pit over there. The large man who the deputies saved was very verbally abusive about the man he called 'Brian', but the remaining nine showed no animosity toward the lawbreaker. Instead they seemed joyous and many of them were hugging despite the stench. It was as if they had been baptized in that crappy water and emerged reborn with all of their sins washed away."

In a grey stone home near the ninth tee, Shannon Erikson ate a croissant and watched the news broadcast from her elegant kitchen.

"The ten survivors, who first resembled stewed prunes, almost looked saintly in their blankets as they were placed in the emergency vehicles headed for Saint Henry's hospital."

The camera zoomed in at the smiling face, which said, "This is Ashley Ludwig with Channel 12. Have a wonderful day!"

Unfortunately for Miss Ludwig, before the camera was turned off she added, "I've never been here in the daytime before."

The doctor's wife, dressed in her black form-fitting exercise outfit, turned off the television and went to tell her husband about the amusing story, but as she reached for the basement doorknob, the front doorbell startled her.

CHAPTER   4

The emergency room at St. Henry's was seldom very busy, but when the victims arrived, still with wet hair, a team of ER doctors and nurses who exchanged their blankets and tacky clothing for smocks welcomed them. After a brief physical examination they were each given a Tetanus shot and the first of three shots for Hepatitis type C during which time Don was warned several times by the medical personnel to watch his language. Before being released, the victims were allowed to shower and then they waited to be interviewed by detectives from the Wood County Sherriff's Department.

The first 'Sewer Celebrity,' as they were now referred, finished his shower and dressed in his own freshly laundered clothing. He had scrubbed vigorously everywhere except for his forehead where the number 12 still showed. When he opened the door to exit the room he was met by two detectives who led him down the hall to a nearby office. He was instructed to sit in the comfortable chair while the detective with the friendly face pulled up a chair and sat across the desk from him. The stern looking detective stood off to the side and introduced himself. "My name is Lieutenant Dan Kalven and this is Sergeant Martin Jaros. He will be conducting the interview."

Sergeant Jaros reached across the desk and shook hands with number 12 who said, "I'm Larry Bertman."

"Larry, how did you end up in that pit with all of those people?"

"Well, it's kind of embarrassing, but he set me up. I live across Poe Road from him and I was mowing my lawn when I saw him drag this long piece of copper wire out into his yard and start to strip off the insulation. I kept my eye on him and after he rolled it up I noticed that he could barely lift it, so I walked over and offered my assistance."

He smiled at the detectives and then continued, "Mind you, we don't get along very well, but with the price of scrap copper these days… well, I just had to find out where he got it from."

Sergeant Jaros asked, "So where did he get it from, Larry?"

Larry shuffled his feet and said; "He said that there was a bunch of it at the old sewage treatment plant in Potterville and that he was only taking it because he was out of work. I helped him carry it to his car and then went home pretending not to be interested, but I was already hooked and a half an hour later I drove to the sewage plant. He must have followed me there, and as I was snooping around he came up behind me with a gun in his hand and put me down in the pit with all of the others. It was dry at the time, but still…"

"Why would he do this to you, Larry?"

Larry confessed, "It was probably my own fault, but I suppose at the time I had my own issues and needed an outlet for my problems. He seemed like such an easy target and I enjoyed picking on him. I'm sorry I did that."

Sergeant Jaros leaned forward and put his arms on the desk then said, "Larry, even though you bullied him, don't you think his actions were a bit extreme?"

"There's more."

"Why would he do this to you, Larry?"

Number 12 lowered his head and said, "Because I shot his kid's dog."

CHAPTER 5

Margaret Shultz took her time showering and getting dressed because she wanted to be the last one interviewed for she had a lot to say and didn't want to inconvenience anyone. She was a changed woman and was determined, from this day on, to always do the right thing. The detectives noticed, like most of the others, she had not washed off the number on her freckled forehead, but wore it like a badge of honor.

Detectives Jaros and Kalven noted that Brian had utilized various techniques in order to capture the ten people in a brief period of time. Usually he appealed to their greed and after discovering what their interests were, used that information to lure them into his trap. Margaret was no exception and her passion was tropical fish. So, an ad was placed in her neighborhood newsletter offering, at a reasonable rate, Kigoma Frontos- rare African blue cichlids.

"I called him the moment I saw the ad trying to contain my excitement. He said he already sold three on Ebay but still had nine left and they would be sold on a first come/first served basis. I said that I would like at least two and offered to pick them up in an hour. Then he gave me directions to the Potterville address and I quickly drove there, but after turning down the gravel road I thought I was at the wrong place. As I tried to turn around a blue car blocked me in and the next thing I knew I was being ushered to that pit at gun point."

16

It was Lieutenant Kalven's turn, "Did he tell you why he was doing that to you?"

"I asked him that and he said, 'You'll have time to think about it,' and that's when I recognized him. It had been 17 years, but he still had the physique of a runner and I'll never forget his serious looking green eyes."

"So you thought about it and what did you come up with?"

"I tried not to think about it, but once the water was turned on, I finally admitted to myself what I had done to deserve that."

The detective nodded for her to go on, she frowned and said, "Besides teaching math, I was then and still am the girl's dean at St. Stephen's High School in Oregon. During the beginning of Brian's senior year, his girlfriend Linda Fejes became pregnant with his child and by late winter it was all too obvious. You have to understand that back in those days a pregnant girl in a parochial school was not tolerated."

"Did you get her expelled?"

"Sort of. I strongly suggested she leave, but thought that he should stay and finish up the year. He had a shot at placing at state in the two mile in track and might have landed a college scholarship, which would have looked good for the school. But, when she left, he transferred with her over to Wade High School. I am a good friend with the counselor over there and received updates from him about them. Brian dropped out of track and got a job working evenings. They both graduated and the very next day they were married at the courthouse. Linda had a baby boy on July 4th, but by then her parents had disowned them and she also moved in with his grandmother. Helen Toth was the grandmother's name. Brian's parents were killed in an automobile accident when he was seven and Helen raised him in her home in the Birmingham neighborhood. Unfortunately, a year later the grandmother died and an uncle forced them out of the house. Where they went from there I didn't know until now."

"Do you think he's finished avenging?"

Before answering, Margaret leaned back in her chair and stretched her back. "I'm sure the others told you about the list, but I really think he only meant to scare us."

Lieutenant Kalven shrugged, "You almost seem grateful, Margaret."

"I am. It was a hard lesson, but he did me a favor and I'm going to be a better person from now on."

CHAPTER 6

Directly after the last interview, the two detectives stayed in the room and shared details with the Sheriff and the two deputies who had freed the ten captives. Then the sheriff made his decision, "Due to the nature of the crime we'll need to bring the Feds in on the case."

He paused and was pleased to see disappointment on the faces of his fellow officers. Then he began to hedge his statement. "Of course, I'll call their main office in Cleveland and then they'll have to call the branch in Toledo, followed by the drive down here to get all of our information. It will waste a lot of valuable time and by then Brian Toth might flee the area or worse, continue his crime spree, but it is what I will do."

The deputies dropped their heads and the detectives looked away from the face of the Sheriff which prompted him to say, "In the mean time, I'll need the deputies to scour the area to find that blue Cavalier and I need you detectives to pick up the search warrant that I ordered from Judge Ashington. Then get out to McKee's Corners and find that list."

The four officers gave the Sheriff a look of admiration followed by a "Yes, sir!" and then hustled from the room.

Back at Channel 12 the station manager had at first kicked himself for sending Miss Ludwig to the crime scene and threw a tirade while waiting for her to return. But, before she showed up he began to receive multiple phone calls and emails supporting the rookie. One viewer said she 'possesses a naiveness that enhances her cuteness' and many others described her as 'hot'. He figured that all of the supporters couldn't be her relatives and friends, so he calmed himself and called his source at the Sheriff Department.

When Ashley and Bob's news van pulled into the station's parking lot, the station manager ran out to meet them. Bob came to a stop in the middle of the parking lot and rolled down his window.

A red faced Ben huffed, "Hey, don't you guys have your cell phones with you?"

Bob blushed and responded, "Sorry Ben, we turned them off during the report and we forgot to turn them back on."

Ashley sheepishly said, "Sorry Ben."

Ben took a deep breath, "Bob, I need you and Ashley to go to McKee's Corners right now. It's a little burg at the intersection of Poe and Milton Roads."

Ashley said, "I know where it is, Ben."

"Okay good. Then show Bob how to get there and continue the captives' story at that site. It's where Brian Toth lives."

CHAPTER 7

Still smiling from the humorous Channel 12 live news report, the doctor's fit wife walked barefoot on the hickory hardwood floor to the foyer, checked her makeup in the wall mirror and peered through the cut glass sidelight. She jumped back when the doorbell rang close to her left ear and nearly fell over the painted milk can that held two oversize umbrellas. She never did like that wedding gift and was now certain to rid herself of it.

Opening the door with her right hand, she used her left to pull her auburn hair behind her ringing ear.

Brian focused on her eyes and said, "I have a package for a Dr. Noah Erikson that requires his signature."

Shannon frowned and said, "What is it?"

Brian, the deliveryman, checked the label, "I don't know what the contents are; only that it was shipped from GGG laboratories."

"He's in the basement reading medical journals. Can't I sign for it? I'm his wife."

The brown uniformed man sighed and toyed with her, "Yes, you can't ma'am. I'm required to witness the doctor's signature."

She turned away from him and said over her shoulder, "Well, alright then, I'll bring him up here."

Before she vacated the foyer, Brian stepped inside, closed and locked the heavy wooden door. She turned and gasped as she saw the handgun pointed at her midsection.

"Settle yourself, Mrs. Erikson, I don't intend to hurt anyone."

Anticipating her question he added, "I only want to talk with the doctor."

CHAPTER 8

Stones flew as the detectives pulled into the driveway of the two story wood sided white house in McKee's Corners. Briskly walking to the front door, they noticed an old woman wearing a pink flowered dress rocking in a chair on the front porch. Although it was a warm day, she wore a shawl over her shoulders.

Detective Martin Jaros spoke first, "Good afternoon, ma'am. Is this Brian Toth's house?"

The eighty-four year old lady stopped rocking and said, "It was his house. Then he sold it back to me late last year, but he does still live here."

Detective Dan Kalven stepped on the porch and said, "Is he here now?"

"No, I saw him leave early this morning. I thought he went to visit his son in the hospital."

Lieutenant Klaven held up a sheet of paper and said, "Ma'am, we have a warrant to search this house…"

She cut him off, "You can call me Martha and please don't break anything. The door is unlocked. Go on in. I've been waiting here for you since I saw the story on my television."

Detective Klaven put the warrant back in his pocket and stepped through the front door into the barren living room. Sergeant Jaros went to follow

23

him when Martha asked, "Is that spunky news girl going to show up too?"

Before Jaros could answer, a bright red van covered with the Channel 12 logo parked next to the officers' vehicle. Martha stood up and said, "I'll bring some cookies over."

He smiled at her and entered the house. The place was void of furniture, rugs and electronic entertainment devices. Only pictures of the suspect, his wife and son adorned the plain walls. One photograph got the attention of Detective Jaros. It was a picture of a weary looking runner who held a toddler with a ribbon and gold medal around the youngster's tiny neck.

"Dan, now I remember why that name sounded so familiar; Brian Toth holds the record for the RUN FROM THE COPS 10K. It was like fifteen years ago, but I'll never forget it. I was working the finish line and the street was lined with people on both sides. When the cheering got louder I looked up to see him come around the corner with two runners right on his heels. For the next two hundred yards he fought off every attempt they made to pass. The crowd was going crazy. The look of agony on his face made me cheer for him. I didn't think he could hold on, but with thirty yards left he surged and broke the tape. The two other runners collapsed, but he just stopped and looked to the sky. I think he was praying. That was when his wife ran out and handed him his son. I'm sure that picture was taken a short time later."

"That's a very interesting story, Martin. Have you found the list yet?"

"No, there's not much here to check in this room. What's the kitchen look like?"

"Not much here either. A card table and a couple of folding chairs. I was under the impression that this list was going to be right out in the open for us to find. Let's check upstairs before we tear anything apart."

CHAPTER 9

Bob exited the van and tended to his camera as Ashley grabbed her microphone and tended to her appearance in the sun visor mirror. She stepped out into the sunlight as Martha approached holding a large plate of chocolate chip cookies with walnuts.

"Hello, would either of you youngsters like to try a cookie. I just baked them this morning."

Bob and Ashley both picked one off of the plate, appraised it and took a bite.

Ashley swallowed and said, "You must be Martha McKee, and I remember you from the bakery booth you had at the Apple Butter Fest."

"I sold pies and cookies there for almost thirty years, but now I just run my town."

"Mrs. McKee I would consider it a personal favor if you would allow me to interview you."

The white haired lady thought about it for a moment and decided, "Come on up on the porch with me and I'll talk with you, but I don't want my picture taken. I haven't fixed my hair yet today; and please, call me Martha."

"It's a deal Martha. You go ahead and sit on the porch. We'll be right up after we send a quick story back to the station."

Martha walked up the few stairs and sat on the rocker with the plate of cookies on her lap as Bob turned his back to her and began filming Ashley.

There were only two bedrooms upstairs. The first looked like it had not been used for a while so both detectives walked into the other. The bed was made and on the dilapidated nightstand sat a Golden Rod tablet with columns of handwritten names. The first name had a line through it. The next two names were scribbled over so much that they were unreadable, but the detectives recognized the names of numbers 4 through 13. Under line 13, a line was drawn with a red marker. Below the line the words 'I Forgive You' were written. Above the line, 'Revenge Is Mine!' At the top of the list printed in bold print was the word COMEUPPANCE.

Showing off her pretty white teeth Ashley began, "Hello again, this is Ashley Ludwig with continuing coverage of today's escapade involving a local man named Brian Toth. Mr. Toth is believed to be the mastermind behind the capture and soaking of ten people in a sewage pit in Potterville. All of the victims were treated and released a short while ago from St. Henry's. Presently, law enforcement officers are searching the home of Brian Toth hoping to find a list that supposedly contains names that Mr. Toth kept. According to the 'Sewer Celebs' whom I spoke with this morning, the list contains 144 names of people who have, to various degrees, offended Mr. Toth. We don't know at this time the whereabouts of Brian Toth, so if anyone has any information relevant to this case please call your local law enforcement agency or Chanel 12. Thank you. We will stay on this story until it is resolved and will bring you live updates as they happen.

Just then the detectives rushed out of the house and as they passed Ashley she asked them if they would stop for a moment to answer a few questions. Bob panned away from the newswoman to record the two officers.

Lieutenant Kalven replied, "No comment," and while getting into their car, both of them looked back to check out Miss Ludwig's posterior.

CHAPTER 10

She stood in the archway leading to the high ceiling living room and spoke in a nervous voice, "If it's money you want, I could write you a check."

With an appraising gaze Brian replied, "I don't want your money. I want to speak with your husband. Take me to him, now."

The doctor's wife apprehensively complied. With the package in his left hand and the gun in his right, he followed her closely as she made her way through the oversized room, into the tiled kitchen toward the basement door. He resisted looking at the granite countertops and kept his focus on her movement while she reached for the doorknob. As they warily descended the carpeted stairs, the sounds of a pinball game grew louder. They entered the game room unnoticed, until Brian slammed the door and said, "Dr. Erikson, your basement is nicer than my house."

A startled Dr. Erikson spun around and said, "What's going on here?"

With the gun pointed at the doctor, Brian set the box on the Ping-Pong table.

The still trembling woman blurted out, "He said he only wanted to talk to you, Noah."

Brian removed his brown cap and tossed it on the table.

With a bewildered glance, the gifted young surgeon recognized the intruder and said, "Brian Toth please put the gun down. I have always been available for consultation."

Brian held on to the gun and said, "If you cooperate fully, I guarantee the safety of your family."

"Okay Brian, what is it you want from us?"

"Doctor, I would like you to take a seat in one of those comfortable chairs there."

Doctor Erikson chose the nearest seat. Then Brian removed the lid from the box and slid it toward the doctor's wife and said, "Take a strand of rope and tie his ankles together.

When she hesitated her husband assured her, "It's okay Shannon. Do what he says. Everything is going to be okay."

She bound his ankles. Then Brian had her repeat the procedure on the doctor's wrists with his arms in front. After Brian checked the knots he secured them with duct tape and then ordered Mrs. Erikson to sit in the leather sofa at the opposite end of the room. Next, Brian bound the doctor to the chair with rope and secured him in place with the duct tape. Finally, he took his black marker from the box, told the doctor to 'hold still' and then proceeded to scribe a very neat number three on his forehead.

The doctor grimaced and said, "Are you done. Can we talk now?"

Brian held the heavy revolver by his side, leaned on the pinball game and said, "I will not lecture you about the death of my wife or the imperative surgery on my son; that will come later. Right now I want to make a trade with you."

Suspiciously the doctor asked, "What kind of trade?"

Brian went on, "I have noticed that there is a definite pecking order in life. That goes not only for people you dislike, but also for people you are very fond of. For example, let's say that you have a daughter named Megan who your wife picks up from kindergarten every weekday at 2:30. I would bet that, forced to make a choice, your wife would sacrifice you to save your daughter."

Doctor number three did not see the look of horror on his wife's face. He held the stare of Brian and said, "That's a reasonable assumption, but you mentioned a trade."

"I also believe that you would sacrifice your partner Dr. Bauhner for the release of your wife."

The married couple looked at each other and as his wife nodded vigorously, Dr. Erikson said, "I would not hesitate for a moment."

CHAPTER 11

Ashley held her smile until Bob lowered the camera. Then she opened the back door of the van while he set the equipment down and secured it in place. Martha again offered the cookies when they reached the porch and Bob went in the house and retrieved the two folding chairs. It became apparent to them that Martha McKee hadn't had company for a while. From the moment they took their seats she turned into a regular chatterbox. She had a mind for details and both Bob and Ashley were grateful for the chairs.

Ashley started with, "Did your ancestors start this town?"

With a look of pride, Martha sat taller in her rocking chair and said, "John McKee settled here back in 1833. The family was well respected as farmers and livestock breeders. I'm all that is left of the McKee family in this area. I don't raise horses and cattle, but I am the self-proclaimed mayor. I rent out these houses and sometimes sell them if I really like the people."

"How did you meet Brian Toth?"

He showed up at my door with his young wife and neither one could have been twenty at the time. She was carrying a year old boy and was desperate for a place to rent. My heart went out to them, not so much that they were reminiscent of the Holy Family, but because they would have reminded me of myself many years earlier if things had turned out differently.

"How do you mean?"

Martha looked at Ashley with sad eyes and explained, "When I was your age I met a man who was five years my elder named Roger. He worked for a lumber company, made regular trips to the big cities like Chicago and seemed like a worldly fellow. I loved the man and thought he felt the same for me. Life was bliss until the day came that I told him I was with child. He seemed to force a smile and made all kinds of promises, but the next day he caught a train and I never saw him again. I went up to the lumberyard and inquired about his whereabouts, but the boys there just laughed at me, I must have looked pretty silly to them.

Ashley's jaw dropped. Then she urged Martha on, "What did you do about the baby?"

"Well, in due time I gave birth to a healthy baby boy that I named Samuel after my grandfather."

Martha's face seemed to glow as she relived the happy times. With a far away look she continued, "He was the joy of my life and I thought the happiness would never end, but it did. It was late winter…"

Ashley and Bob remained silent and allowed Martha to finish her story.

Martha hesitated and then went on, "Little Samuel was three years old when he caught pneumonia. For two weeks he struggled with it, but one night as I held him in my arms, he died. I buried him in a sunny spot on the other side of the ravine there."

Bob got up and walked to the far side of the van. Ashley wiped the tears from her eyes and said, "I'm so sorry Martha."

Martha reached out and put her hand on Ashley's and said. "I didn't want to make you cry honey, but I needed to tell you that story so that you would understand how I felt for Brian and Linda and their son, Alex."

A composed Ashley said, "So I'm guessing they became your adoptive family?"

"Very much so. I babysat Alex whenever they'd let me and helped them out however I could, but they helped me too whenever I needed a hand with fixing something on the buildings."

Ashley changed gears, "Martha did you know what Brian was up to this morning?"

"I didn't know until I heard his name mentioned in the background by someone during your news story. He kept talking about the big event that he was training for, but I thought he meant the Glass City Marathon or something."

Ashley shifted in her seat and said, "You know Brian very well. What made him do it?"

34

Martha spoke softer, "Brian had a lot of anger in him. For starters, his wife passed away last year and then his son got sick. He had so many medical bills that he sold just about everything of any value, including the house. He became very cynical and before long all he did was go to work, run and visit his son in the hospital. All I can tell you is that I love him like a son. I'm getting tired now, so I'm going to go home and lay down. If you need more information about Brian, try the house two doors down. A young man named Nathan lives there. I'll bet he'll talk to you."

CHAPTER   12

The bound Dr. Erikson said, "So how do you propose I get Dr. Bauhner to agree to come over here now?"

Brian pondered the question and then said, "Maybe you should call him and invite him over for whatever excuse you can come up with. I know he's nearby because he had an early tee time on this course today."

"You have obviously done your research."

"You have no idea, doctor."

The shapely doctor's wife waved her hand in the air and said, "How about if I call him and say that I'm all alone and I need something heavy moved?"

Both men gave her a blank stare and then finally Dr. Erikson had an idea. "I know. I have this Revolutionary War sword that my father left me. I never liked it because it scared me as a child and one of the reasons I kept it was that I knew Richard would love to have it. I always teased him that I was going to donate it to the Wood County Museum. I'll just call him and offer to sell it to him."

Brian nodded, "That should work."

Shannon Erikson bounced up from her chair, pulled her cell phone from the pocket of her black tights and said, "I'll dial for you, Noah."

As she stepped towards her husband, Brian noticed that she hit speed dial before holding the phone to his ear.

A minute after Ashley's update from McKee's Corners was aired, the phone began to ring at the Wood County Sheriff's Department. Callers swore they saw Brian Toth at the hardware store, in a bar and on the bike trail. One man claimed to be Brian.

A few asked if the suspect had been caught yet, but most inquired about being on the list. An older woman made one such call from Toledo. The officer noticed the two detectives enter the room and put her on hold.

"Hey Jaros, before you talk to the sheriff, can you tell me if a Mrs. Coughlin is on the list."

Lieutenant Kalven answered for him, "If you're talking to that Channel 12 news girl, we can't divulge any evidence at this time."

"No Dan, I'm not speaking with Ashley Ludwig; not even close. There's a frightened old woman on the line who thinks she might be on the list."

Detective Martin Jaros scanned the yellow tablet and said, "Yes she's on here, number 127, but don't tell her."

The detectives proceeded to the sheriff's office and the officer took Mrs. Coughlin off hold.

"Sorry I took so long, but you'll be happy to know that I did not see your name on the list, Mrs. Coughlin. Can you tell me why you thought you might have been on the list?"

FLASHBACK #2

In the second row of wooden desks, a small nine-year-old boy who sported a blonde crew cut sat on his wooden, tall-backed chair. He squirmed for as long as he could and then again stood and slowly approached the fourth grade teacher who sat at her large desk in front of the black slate chalkboard.

When she looked up with a sour expression he softly said, "Mrs. Coughlin can I please go to the restroom?"

She sternly scolded him, "Brian, the entire class went a couple of hours ago. Didn't you go then?"

He shifted from foot to foot, "No, I didn't have to go then. I only got a drink of water, but I have to really go now."

She gave him a disapproving look and said, "Go back to your seat and sit down. Maybe next time you'll follow orders better."

Young Brian Toth shuffled back to his seat and sat down. A short time later his bladder emptied and urine soaked his navy blue corduroy pants and then ran down the chair legs and formed a puddle on the bare hardwood floor.

When Mrs. Coughlin spotted what the horrified child had done, she rolled her eyes at him.

There was a pause on the phone line and then Mrs. Coughlin said, "I'd rather not speak about the incident. I only called to see if I was in any danger."

"Let me assure you Mrs. Coughlin that every effort is being made to relieve the citizens of the problem."

CHAPTER 13

The Sheriff sat and assessed the hand written pages on his desk as the two detectives stood nearby. Below the red line, he was surprised to see more than a few recognizable names and became more concerned. Finally, he looked up at the men and queried, "Can we trust this guy not to harm anyone below the line?"

The two detectives looked at each other and then Martin said, "I have a feeling that we can trust him in that regard. We are concerned about the top three names though."

Dan interjected, "You may be familiar with the number one name. Theodore Auffendor was a victim of suicide shortly before Christmas last year. No foul play was suspected; he shot himself with his own gun and left a short note to his wife stating he 'couldn't live like this anymore'."

Martin pointed at the indecipherable names of numbers two and three and said, "Neither one of us can make out who those two are. Maybe the lab can read them for us."

There was a knock on the door and then another officer entered the room and said, "Sir, a car matching the description of the suspect's has been located at Wintergarden Park."

The sheriff handed the tablet to the deputy and said, "Take this to the lab and see if they can figure out the names on the second and third line.

Then get a list of addresses of all these people and see if any of them reside in one of the neighborhoods adjacent to the park."

The officer scurried out and the sheriff said to the detectives, "You two get over to the park and check out that car."

Doctor Richard Bauhner sat at the bar of the clubhouse and drank his second beer. Although it was a pleasant late spring day, his game hadn't gone very well. While he had searched for the second ball that was hit into the water, he observed an attractive pair of women putting on the 18th green. That had been enough justification for him to call it a day. After he had made some lame excuse to the other three guys in the group, he waved and said that maybe he would see them at the bar after they finished up. Then he had high-tailed it to the clubhouse just in time to intercept the women.

They had accepted his drink offer, but when he made a lewd suggestion involving the three of them, they walked out. Unfazed, he ordered another beer. His attention was drawn to the television mounted above the bottles of liquor when the pretty newswoman's voice mentioned the name of Brian Toth. As he reached for another handful of peanuts from the glass bowl on the polished bar, his cell phone rang. He looked to see who the caller was then answered it.

"Hello, Shannon, what can I do for you?"

Doctor Erikson was elated that he had gotten through to him and said, "Actually, Richard, this is Noah and I want to do something for you. Are you in town?"

Doctor Bauhner spun around on his bar stool and said, "Yah, I'm at the clubhouse, what's up?"

"Shannon and I are going to redecorate the place and we want to know if you are still interested in the sword?"

"Ah, yes. Yes I am."

"Well then, if you can find your way over here before I change my mind and donate it to the museum, you can have it for the last price that you offered."

"Gee, Noah, don't give it to the museum, I'll be right over. I'm driving the cart so it will take a little longer, but I'll be there soon."

"Okay, I'll wait for you. Just come in the front door. We'll be down in the game room, Richard."

The doctor paid his bar tab, left a generous tip and then hopped onto his golf cart and as he headed towards the Erikson residence he said aloud, "I think my luck is about to change."

CHAPTER   14

Ashley watched as Martha descended the steps and cautiously walked back across the lawn to her own house. Bob agreed to stay in the van when Ashley hiked over to the house on the other side of Martha's, but he insisted that she have her phone ready to alert him in the event of an emergency. She agreed, and then walked across the sunlit lawns to the house that looked as if it had recently received a fresh coat of white paint. When she knocked on the door she could hear a Neil Young song playing somewhere within the well kept home. A pleasant breeze played with her hair as she knocked louder and soon the door opened and revealed a six-foot, twenty seven year old muscular man with wavy longish dark brown hair, wearing sweat pants, a tee shirt and sneakers. He appeared a little groggy, but woke up quickly as his eyes focused on Miss Ludwig in her long sleeved white blouse and black high-waisted pencil skirt.

"Why, hello, what can I do for you?"

"Hi, I'm Ashley Ludwig. I was just speaking with Martha McKee about Brian Toth and she told me your name and suggested that I also talk to you to get a different perspective."

Nathan Kovacs pointed a finger at her and said, "Oh, you're the latest Channel 12 newswoman. I just caught a glimpse of you on the TV and I have to say, you're even more attractive in person. Would you like to come in and sit down?"

She rewarded the compliment with a smile and then said, "Actually, I sat a long time on Martha's porch and prefer to stand outside and enjoy this gorgeous weather."

Pretending to be hurt he said, "Okay, Ashley."

Ashley added, "And would you mind if I have my cameraman record our conversation to be used later in a news story?"

He considered the request and said, "What did Martha do?"

Ashley sighed and admitted, "She didn't want to be filmed because she thought her hair was too messy, but your hair looks good."

His face reddened slightly, "Thanks, even though I know that you are stroking me. But, I don't think I want to be recorded either, maybe some other time. However, I will answer any questions you have."

"Alright Nathan, have you known Brian very long?"

"I met Brian about nine years ago at Owens College when I sat next to him in my electrical classes. We hit it off really well and when I said that I was looking for a place to rent, he turned me on to Martha."

"Does he have any social problems?"

"There are a few people he doesn't get along with, but usually those types of people haven't taken the time to get to know him or they are envious of him for whatever reason. It's probably because he is in tremendous shape and they are not."

"Nathan, from what I have gathered so far today, Brian has been under relentless pressure. From the death of Linda and the hospitalization of Alex, he has gone from being a carefree guy to a very distraught man."

"No doubt about it, Ashley. He was very nervous about the heart transplant, but afterwards he was ecstatic when the doctors told him that the operation was a success and that a complete recovery was predicted. The good news was short-lived though when an infection set in and then Brian became depressed. I know from our conversations that he was having a hard time sleeping so he stepped up his training just to wear himself out, plus he ran three marathons the past year. He said that the running helped to relieve the stress and he felt almost normal at times."

Ashley squinted slightly and said, "Was there any particular person or event that would set him off?"

Nathan pursed his lips then decided, "Besides Linda's death, something happened in the hospital which really upset him."

"Maybe he held the hospital responsible."

"No, I asked him that and he said he needed more time to think about that issue, so I felt he was disturbed about something else, but he wouldn't tell me what it was."

FLASHBACK #3

After the nurse checked on her, she left Linda's bedside and Brian and his wife had total privacy in the low lighted room. A week earlier, just when things looked bleak, a heart donor was found in the form of a twenty three year old male motorcyclist victim. Doctors Bauhner and Erikson had successfully exchanged the healthy organ for Linda's deteriorated heart. Brian and all involved were exuberant for a few days when huge steps toward her recovery were being made. Then the cheerful atmosphere began to fade when an infection occurred and over the last couple of days, feverish Linda alternated between states of consciousness. As he stood at the side of her bed watching her sleep, he marveled at her beauty even at this stage of her life. When he brushed back strands of brown hair from her forehead, she opened her bright blue eyes and seemed amazingly awake.

For the first time in two days he heard her voice, "Have you been here long?"

He smiled at her and said, "About one thousand Hail Marys."

"How is our son doing?"

"Other than worrying about you, he is doing extremely well. His name was on the honor roll again and you are looking at the father of the regional champion. He didn't want to go, but I told him that you would want him to be there, so of course he went.

Linda appeared enthralled as she always did when Brian described the activities of Alexander.

Brian savored the look. Then went on, "Right before the gun went off, he glanced my way and I told him to 'make your mom proud'. You should have seen him. He controlled the race from start to finish. I just hope he saved a little for State next week. I think he has a chance to place."

Brian reached into his pants pocket and retrieved the first place medal from the regional meet and showed it to Linda.

"Alex was here earlier. He wanted to put this around your neck."

At first Linda appeared pleased. A somber look took over as she said, "Brian, I'm getting tired again, but I want to tell you something, so please don't interrupt me."

With a quizzical expression Brian said, "Okay, what is it?"

She gave him a worried look and then took a deep breath and began, "A couple of years ago. It was a Friday. Alex was staying at a friend's house and you were working the second shift. I had planned a romantic night for us once you came home from work. Candles were lit throughout the house, soft music was playing, I made some hors d'oeuvres and a bottle of wine was being chilled. You were supposed to work until midnight and then I was going to surprise you. So, about 10 o'clock I sampled the wine while I took a bubble bath. When I was putting on my negligee, I thought I heard someone pull into the driveway so I put on my housecoat and noticed a man looking in the side window. When I went to make sure that the doors were locked, he knocked at the front door. I peeked over the curtain and saw Ted's truck parked there."

Brian stopped her, "Ted from church?"

"No, I'm referring to my sister's husband, Ted."

"You didn't open the door did you?"

"Please don't interrupt, let me finish."

Brian bit his tongue and she continued, "He reeked of beer and said that he only wanted to use the bathroom, and then he would leave. So, I let him in and he used the bathroom, but when he came out he had my glass of wine in his hand and he said 'It looks like you're throwing a party for me'. I told him that you would be home soon and that he needed to leave. He drank the wine in one gulp and went to the front door, but instead of leaving he locked it and turned around with an ugly sneer on his face. I tried to run towards the back door, but he grabbed my wrist and pulled my housecoat off. He was too strong for me, I couldn't stop him; he was too heavy.

After he left I put away the food and wine and blew out all of the candles making the house look normal. Then I took a long hot shower and went to bed. When you came home I pretended to be asleep. I'm sorry, Brian."

Brian trembled with rage on the inside, but externally he insisted that she had done nothing wrong. He changed the subject to her improving health and their wonderful future together. However, as he left the hospital and walked to his car the gears in his mind turned and he began to make plans.

CHAPTER   15

Ashley unconsciously took a half step toward Nathan. "Do you consider Brian to be a vengeful man?"

"He once told me, 'You can't accomplish anything when you're sad; it's only when you're angry that you can get the job done'."

"Do you believe that?"

"Brian used to be such a hard working, happy go lucky guy, but after Linda died, he changed some. He was quieter, more focused and oblivious to everything else. Even our conversations changed. There was no longer the banter between us and he became more serious. Brian worked as much as he could to pay the medical bills. He even sold his house back to Martha and a lot of his possessions. He seemed afraid. When he found out that Alex had inherited his wife's heart disease, it brought him to his knees.

"Do you think Brian is capable of murder?"

"Wow, I hope not. But lately he seemed tense and preoccupied. The last time I talked with him, our conversation was very short. Just before he left he gave me a hard look and said, 'Above all things, I admire loyalty'."

"You speak of him with admiration in your voice. Do you try to emulate his philosophies?"

"Ashley, I have always considered myself to be an adventure seeker. I never got too serious with a woman and wondered how Brian could stand watching Linda fade away like that. As I initially watched it unfold, I thought that I wouldn't be able to handle the situation he was in, but when I witnessed Brian's love for her, I decided it would be worth the risk of losing."

"I would love to interview him." Ashley thought aloud.

Nathan said with a smirk, "Do you want me to call him?"

Ashley seemed to glow, "Yes. I can't believe that I hadn't thought of that. Do you think he'll answer?"

"Let's find out."

Nathan went into his home to locate his cell phone. He soon returned to an anxious looking Ashley with the phone held to his ear.

"He's not answering. Probably has it turned off."

Just then the phone in Ashley's hand began to ring and Nathan teased her, "That's probably Brian trying to get a hold of you now."

Ashley looked at her phone and saw that it was Bob calling.

"Hello, Bob. What's the good news?"

"The good news is that Ben just received a tip that Brian Toth's car has been located at the nature center in Wintergarden Park and that he wants us to scoot right over there and do another live update. Are you finished over there yet?"

"I'm wrapping it up here Bob. I'll see you in a minute or two."

Nathan gave her the look of a sad puppy when she said that she had to leave. "Ashley, you are quite charming. Would you go to lunch with me sometime?"

Ashley looked pleased and before she turned and walked to the van she said, "Maybe."

Nathan watched her until she was out of sight. He said to no one in particular, "She said 'maybe'."

CHAPTER 16

Sometimes on restless nights, the solutions would come to him in his dreams, but usually they would appear when he ran. He suspected that more blood flowed to his brain at that time or that some kind of endorphin was released to elevate his intelligence. Often he would wake up in the middle of the night and write down his thoughts on a note pad that was kept in his nightstand. He would later read the new information while changing into his running gear. With the additional data entered into his brain, he would begin his run and sort through the new clues to determine what punishment would be appropriate. Sometimes his list of the 144 offenders would be shuffled and reordered, but the top twenty-five or so always stayed the same. You would have to do something really nasty to move up into that group.

Shannon Erikson returned to her seat with the cell phone. Brian walked over and sat next to her with the .44 resting on his lap.

Doctor Erikson broke the silence, "What did you write on my forehead?"

Brian remained silent, so Shannon answered the question, "He wrote the number three."

"What does that mean?" her husband asked.

"Noah, before he came to the door, I was on my way down here to tell you about the news report from Potterville. Apparently, there is an old sewage plant there and this guy had several people held there in some kind of large container this morning. The people had numbers on their foreheads, just like you do."

"Okay. So I'm number three."

Bolstered with the knowledge that she would soon be released, Shannon turned to Brian and asked, "Who's number one?"

FLASHBACK #4

As the green Ford pickup truck pulled out of the driveway, Brenda stood on the lawn and waved to her husband. Ted would be gone for a week on his annual deer-hunting trip to Pennsylvania and although she felt jubilant about his absence, she would not admit it to herself.

He drove north until he came to the Ohio Turnpike. After receiving his fare ticket at the entrance booth, he pointed the truck east, put on the cruise control and opened a cold beer. He relished the thought of what lay ahead of him: the camaraderie, the partying and maybe even a little deer hunting. Somewhere near Cleveland as he left the rest area with an empty bladder and a full fuel tank, his cell phone rang. He didn't recognize the caller's number, but he answered it anyhow and was rewarded with a sexy woman's voice.

"Hello, is this Ted?"

"The one and only."

"Ted, my name is Amber. Your generous friends from Pennsylvania have convinced me that, since you're such a great guy, I would want to meet you."

"Oh really, what do you have in mind?"

Well, I thought you might want to start off with a drink."

"Sure, where can I meet you?"

"If you get off at the Warren exit and head south a mile, you'll see a motel on the right called Tucker Inn. It's a yellow brick building hidden by a lot of pine trees. I'll be the redhead in the lounge, drinking a beer."

Ted accelerated a bit and thought that this may be the best hunting trip yet. He almost missed the turn into the motel, but recovered and found that there were ample parking places. During the walk to the lounge, he didn't recognize any of the few parked cars and felt relieved.

Amber was drinking a bottle of Yuengling when he approached her. She had on a slinky yellow top over jeans and black high heels. When he arrived next to her, she smiled at him and said, "You must be Ted."

"That makes you Amber."

"Are you thirsty, Ted?"

"A little."

"Are you hungry, Ted?"

"Not for food."

She reached into her pocket and produced a room key and said, "Well, then, why don't you head down to room number 7 and make yourself comfortable? I'll have some drinks made and bring them down to you."

Before Amber arrived with the cocktails, Ted searched the room for any recording devices. When he was satisfied that the room was safe he sat on the bed. A short time later she tapped on the door with her shoe. As he let her in, she handed him a full glass and said, "I hope you like Crown Royal."

"I love it."

She took a sip of her drink and said, "Why don't you sit on the bed and watch while I get out of these clothes."

"Great idea."

As Amber slowly disrobed, Ted sat wide-eyed on the edge of the bed gulping his drink. She began with her shoes, followed by her top. Next, she turned around and removed her bra, but as she stepped out of her jeans she saw that he had already passed out on the bed. Before tossing her jeans on the unconscious Ted, she removed her cell phone from her pocket. He didn't even flinch so she called the number.

"Hey Randy, this is Amber."

"That was fast."

"He's out cold. Come on over."

Amber opened the door for Randy wearing only a purple thong. Randy carried a small duffle bag into the room and looked at sleeping Ted and then back to Amber then said, "He's going to miss a heck of a party."

Ashley put her hands on her hips and said, "Did you want to take some pictures now?"

"I did bring a camera."

They undressed the sleeping drunk and put him in various poses on the bed with Amber while Randy took several photographs. When he felt he had enough pictures, Randy paid her the agreed upon sum of money. She dressed and stuffed the cash into her pocket and said, "Well, he should be out all night and he won't remember a thing in the morning. I hope this prank goes well for you."

"I'm sure it will. Thanks. And remember, this never happened."

He opened the door for her to leave and said, "I'm guessing that 'Amber' isn't your real name."

She smiled and as she stepped outside. "I'll bet that 'Randy' isn't your real name either."

"Touché."

Brian shut and locked the door and made sure that the curtains were still closed tightly and opened his duffle bag. He laid Ted on his back and using nylon rope, tied him spread eagle to the bed frame. With duct tape, he gagged and blindfolded the heavy man. When he was satisfied that the clod was fully restrained, he reached into his bag and pulled out a Burdizzo. Normally used on farm animals, the castration tool is used to crush the blood vessels connected to the testicles. Brian carefully placed the business end of the clamping tool around the blood vessels of the dozing man's left testicle. When he was certain that the placement was exact, he used both hands and squeezed with purpose. The unconscious man lurched, but did not awaken. Brian repeated the procedure on the right side and returned the tool to the duffle bag. He removed the rope and tape from the sleeping gelding. After checking to be certain that he had everything he had arrived with, Brian tucked Ted in for the night, turned out the lights and left.

CHAPTER   17

Without looking for traffic, the tipsy Dr. Bauhner drove his golf cart from the designated path onto the roadway. He did not admire the landscaped newly built homes, but instead sped to his destination. As he skidded to a halt just before the Ericson's garage door, he looked back and chuckled at the tire marks left on the previously unstained concrete driveway. Then he strolled to the front door, rang the doorbell and stepped inside.

When Brian heard the doorbell, he ordered Shannon to play the pinball game until Dr. Bauhner stepped into the game room. Brian remained seated and kept the gun out of sight. Muffled footstep sounds increased as the happy man descended the carpeted stairway. When the doctor entered the room he said, "What's the score Shannon?"

She stopped playing as both Eriksons looked over at Brian who stood and pointed the gun at the newcomer.

Dr. Bauhner looked disappointed and said to the gunman, "Don't tell me you're from the Wood County Historical Museum."

Dr. Erikson answered for him, "Good one, Richard. Actually, this is Brian Toth and he wants to talk to us."

Richard looked back and forth between the two men as Brian spoke up, "First things first. Shannon, tie him up like you did your husband."

The doctor complied and as Shannon bound his ankles and wrists, she whispered in his ear, "I guess you need to be careful what you ask for."

When she finished, Brian had her take a seat. He checked the knots and secured the ropes with the duct tape. He used the remaining rope and duct tape to fasten Richard to his chair. Lastly, he took off the cap of the black marker and scribed a number two on Dr. Bauhner's forehead.

"Can I leave now?" Shannon said.

"Not just yet. I have to write a letter for you to deliver."

"I have to pick up Megan soon."

Brian ignored her and removed a clean sheet of paper from his clipboard, sat it on the edge of the Ping-Pong table and began to write. When he finished, he read it and taped the ends shut with narrow strips of the duct tape.

"Okay, Mrs. Erikson you can pick up your daughter now."

Shannon hopped up and Brian handed her the letter.

"After you leave the kindergarten, I want you to deliver this to the Bowling Green Chief of Police."

Shannon examined the exterior of the letter and said, "It doesn't look very professional."

Brian pointed her towards the steps and said,
"I'm really not a deliveryman."

CHAPTER 18

The area around the blue Cavalier was secured with yellow plastic police tape. The hood, trunk and all four doors were wide open. There was an officer from the lab inside the vehicle and another perusing the trunk. Both were looking for clues they hoped would provide information regarding the present location of Brian Toth or his current intentions. The Bowling Green patrol officer who found the car, sat in his vehicle and talked with another city cop whose automobile was parked next to his, but pointed in the opposite direction. Detectives Kalven and Jaros stood next to trunk of the suspect's car and discussed the contents.

"There's a clue for your nose to solve, Martin," said Lieutenant Kalven.

"I'm going to go out on a limb here and say that the suspect took off those smelly clothes there, freshened up and, this part is mere speculation, put on clean clothes," said Sergeant Jaros.

"I concur. He may have ridden away in another car or rode a bike, but I have a hunch that he is still in the area."

"Dan, maybe he changed into his running shoes and ran away from here."

"Possibly, but whatever he did, I have to believe that he would want to stick around close to the hospital and try to see his son before he is arrested."

Detective Kalven looked up and saw the pesky red Channel 12 news van parked on the edge of the lane. He glanced behind him at the nature center and said, "I'll be right back, Martin. I need to make use of the facilities here and then I'll report in and see if the lab has deciphered those two names yet."

Before he saw her, Detective Jaros smelled her perfume and then heard her voice. As he turned around, the sight of the perky young lady delighted him.

Standing with her back to the cordoned off area, she began. "Good afternoon. This is Ashley Ludwig with another live Channel 12 update. I'm standing in Wintergarden Park and behind me is the automobile believed to be the escape vehicle used this morning by the suspect Brian Toth. If you have been following today's top story you have already heard about the ten victims who were traumatized by Mr. Toth this morning at the abandoned Potterville Wastewater Treatment Plant. Eventually, all ten were released physically unharmed. It is not known if the crime spree is over, but the police are one step closer to solving this case.

Using her free hand, Ashley brushed back the hairs that were tickling her nose and continued. "After my last report in McKee's Corners, I had the opportunity to speak with two of Brian Toth's neighbors. By his actions this morning, many viewers may have pictured Mr. Toth as just another cruel criminal. But, after listening to Martha McKee's and Nathan Kovacs' depictions of the man, I was given a glimpse of the highs and lows of his life. Brian Toth has been on both ends of cruelty. Although circumstances have not always been very friendly to him, he was described to me as a very loving husband and father who worked hard to provide for his family. Here is a little recent history to help you understand his world. Last fall, Brian's wife passed away a few days after receiving a heart transplant. Within a week following her funeral, their son was diagnosed with the same aggressive heart disease. Following that, Mr. Toth was laid off from his place of employment. He has since sold most of his possessions including his home to pay the huge medical expenses."

Ashley thought she sounded a little shook up, so she paused and took a deep breath before she continued, "None of these hardships can justify what he did to those people this morning, but they do explain them somewhat. Most of the victims have already forgiven him and so far, he has not physically harmed anyone. Brian, if you're listening, please turn yourself in. They say that time heals all wounds…"

Bob gave her five seconds and when she didn't speak again, he shut the camera off.

Detective Jaros was so engrossed in Ashley's story that he didn't notice Lieutenant Kalven standing next to him.

"So Martin, have you located anymore clues?"

"You have to admit Dan, compared to the odor coming from the trunk of that car, Miss Ludwig smells pretty good."

Lieutenant Kalven sampled the air. "I'll bet, that tonight you'll jack off thinking about her."

"A gentleman never tells."

"Come on, we need to go back to the office. The lab has something for us and the Feds are in town now."

CHAPTER 19

Bound in the basement game room, the two doctors sat quietly and felt anxious like two caged chickens at a farmer's market. Brian sat across from them and stared at the floor as he gathered his thoughts, and then he began, "After this morning's events you may think that this is about revenge; that I hold you responsible for my wife's death. I do not."

Both doctors looked a little relieved, but still flinched whenever Brian would unconsciously point the gun in their direction.

"After much reflection, I was able to let go. When I brought her to the hospital, she was fading fast, but a miracle happened. A donor was found and you guys came through for us, until something went wrong. That damn infection changed everything. I tried very hard to hold you accountable, but I couldn't."

Very softly Brian said, "I forgive you."

The doctors looked at him with hope in their eyes as he continued.

"I also want to thank you for the flowers that you sent for Linda's funeral."

Brian's mind drifted back to the past All Saint's Day.

FLASHBACK #5

The scent of the multicolored mums saturated the air around the twenty people who gathered close under the canopy trying to avoid the drizzling rain. The sullen grey skies matched the expressions on the faces of the people dressed in black who watched Father Matt sprinkle the coffin with holy water. They remembered the words of his homily and they felt slightly better. Brian felt numb. Standing next to his son Alex, the events of the past month rushed through his mind. There was the initial fear when he was informed that an organ transplant was mandatory for continued life. Next, the successful heart operation brought elation, which was followed by infection, fever, coma and death. At times the grief overwhelmed him. One moment he had his emotions under control, the next he would sob uncontrollably as the sadness took him by surprise, like a sneeze.

The rest of the short ceremony was a blur and when it had ended, Brian found himself walking back to the cars next to his wife's sister. When they reached her red Corvette, Brian tried to smile. "The women from St. Louis in Bowling Green are having a wake in the gymnasium. I'm sure the food is good. You're welcome to come if you'd like."

Other than having darker hair and being slightly taller than her sister, Brenda looked very similar to Linda. She gave him a brief hug and said, "I'm sorry Brian. I told Ted I would come home right after the funeral."

Brian felt the anger building up in him, but kept it to himself.

"So where is your husband today?"

"He said he had to stay home and get ready for his hunting trip, even though it is not until a week from this Saturday."

CHAPTER 20

When the silver SUV turned down the alley next to the Bowling Green Police Department, the curly haired kindergartener wondered aloud, "Where are we going Mommy?"

Retrieving the letter from the center console Shannon said, "I have to give somebody this letter, Megan."

"But this isn't the post office."

The doctor's wife parked the gas-guzzler in back at the bank parking lot. Then with her daughter in tow, she walked with the letter to the front of the renovated police station. Still dressed in the tight outfit that accented her curves, she was gawked at by the men who passed by her. She basked in the attention. After climbing the front steps of the three story, red brick building, she entered and using the directory on the wall, located the Chief's office. As they walked to the office, they passed a couple of officers wearing their dark uniforms. The wide-eyed five year old clung to her mother's side as the sounds of footsteps echoed from the marble floors. A young well groomed officer met them at the door.

"Hello, Ma'am. What can I do for you?"

Shannon smiled and said, "I have a letter for your Chief."

"Right this way," said the officer.

He turned on his heel and they followed, stopping in front of the Chief's desk. The Chief was reading when they entered and without looking up, he spoke with annoyance, "Yes, what is it?"

"Chief, this woman has a letter for you."

The Chief sat up straight and, using an index finger, pushed his glasses to the proper position on his face. Megan hid behind her mom. In a much more pleasant tone, the Chief said, "Who is the letter from?"

Megan felt like she was Dorothy visiting the Wizard and wanted to leave, but Shannon stepped forward, dragging her daughter and handed him the letter.

"The letter is from Brian Toth. He has a gun and is in the basement of our home, holding my husband and his partner hostage."

"What is your husband's name?"

"He's Dr. Noah Erikson and the other guy is Dr. Richard Bauhner. Can I leave now?"

"You can't go home, obviously. Is there somewhere else you can go?"

"My mother lives on Clark Street. I'll take Megan there."

"Okay good. But, first go with this officer and he'll take down some more information from you."

After the three had left the room, the chief ordered the captain of the police to his office. Then he cautiously opened the letter and began to read it.

CHAPTER   21

"I need you guys. My son is coming to the end of his time on the waiting list. I saw him last night and he looked terrible. Is everything being done to locate a heart for him?"

Dr. Bauhner looked tired when he said, "Is that why we are here?"

"We are here doctor, to discuss our options."

"You didn't think we could do this at our office?" said Dr. Erikson.

"I wanted your complete attention and I felt that if your lives were on the line, you would be more apt to make an extreme effort to help Alex. Under these conditions you might be more forthcoming with the truth. This way, I will have exhausted all options and then I will be able to make the final decision."

Both doctors were afraid of the contents of Brian's statement and neither asked him for an explanation. Instead Dr. Erikson tried to steer the conversation toward a happier memory.

"The waiting is sometimes the most difficult part for transplant patients and their families. Other than the heart, your son's body is in superb condition. Didn't he do really well at the state championship last fall?"

FLASHBACK #6

It was a cool morning in Columbus and there was dew on the grass at Scioto Downs on the first Saturday of November. On the strength of Alex Toth's first place finish at the regional, the entire Otsego high school cross-country team qualified for the state championship. The sixteen best teams in the state had performed their warm up runs, stretched out and stripped down to only their light-weight tops, shorts, socks and shoes. The Knights wore black and white with orange trimmed uniforms and were surrounded by teams with every color combination imaginable. With only a few minutes remaining before the start of the race, the team stayed close to their designated chalked starting position. Assistant coach Brian stayed back off the line about twenty yards and allowed the head coach to perform the pre-race tradition, consisting of a prayer and a pep talk. Well familiar with the course, Brian knew if he ran as the crow flies, he would be able to be at the mile markers just before the lead pack arrived. An announcement was made requesting all coaches and other non-participants to clear the course and Alex jogged back to speak with his father. Brian didn't mention the tragedy of the past week. Instead, he was all business.

"Alex, this isn't your first big race. Last year as a sophomore, you finished twenty-second and I believe that now you are in good enough shape to receive first team All-Ohio honors if you run a smart race."

Alex, who had been staring at his shoes, looked at Brian and said, "Dad, when does the pain go away?"

"I don't know, son."

"Do you think Mom is proud of me?"

All Brian could do was nod and as he turned and began running towards the first mile marker, his eyes welled-up. Behind him, he heard the starting pistol and looked back to see the mass of colors blend into an adrenalin primed stampede.

Brian waited at the mile mark counting runners and looking at his watch. When Alex ran by with his head down at 5:05, Brian shouted at him, "Stop feeling sorry for yourself!"

At the 2-mile mark, Brian was pleased with what he saw. Alex looked strong and was running smoothly unlike some of the struggling runners around him. He had a look of determination on his face and when he went by in fifth position just under ten minutes, Brian shouted, "Make a decision, Alex."

Near the finish line, Brian glanced at his watch and when he looked up, a close pack of four runners materialized. His heart leaped when he realized that Alex was leading them home. As the runners got closer, the spectators grew louder. Brian could see that one of the four was fading and Alex was pulling away from the other two. However, with a tenth of a mile left, Alex eased up and was passed by one of the prep runners. Brian was very satisfied with his son's effort and placement, but a little concerned with his condition near the finish line. He found his son sitting on the grass.

"Alex that was beautiful. You ran like a warrior today."

Alex looked up at his father with fear in his eyes and said, "I'm really tired."

Brian pulled him up by his wrists and said, "You ought to be; you set a PR today."

"Dad, my heart hurts."

"You'll feel better in a little while," Brian said as he hugged his son and wondered whom he was trying to convince.

CHAPTER 22

Dear Chief,

By now you have heard of me. I am desperate, yet still rational. Everyone who I have cared about the most in my life has died or is dying. Time is running out for my son. Currently I am reviewing our options with two of the best heart surgeons known. I am hoping for a miracle. (Maybe, the media attention will somehow move us up on the waiting list.) Your cooperation and patience is appreciated. I will resolve this situation as quickly as possible. Please do not raid the house. I do not want to harm either one of these important citizens.

Brian Toth

When the captain entered the chief's office, he was handed the letter and as he read it, the Chief used his computer to obtain the address of Dr. Erikson.

"Captain, we have a hostage situation at one of the homes on the golf course. This is the guy that the Sheriff's Department has been looking for all day. He was last seen in the basement game room in the home of Dr. Noah Erikson. The address is 1955 Candy Land Lane. Besides Dr. Erikson, Brian Toth is holding a Dr. Richard Bauhner at gunpoint. Get your men over there and cordon off the area. Stay away from the windows, do not enter the residence and report back when the area is secured."

When detectives Kalven and Jaros entered the sheriff's office, they were introduced to Agent Lurk who sat in a chair off to the side of the desk. The sheriff informed them that he had passed along all information to the federal officer and that the lab had deciphered some of the letters of the two obscured names on the list. He assured them that it was only a matter of time until they would know the identities of the two potential victims. As Agent Lurk was about to speak, the sheriff received a call from the Bowling Green Chief of Police. After exchanging the usual pleasantries, the Chief told the Sherriff that he had just obtained information on the Brian Toth case. The sheriff informed the chief of the three other officers in the room with him and then switched to speakerphone. After being introduced to the FBI agent, the Chief shared with them the recent acquired information including the contents of the letter and the location of the suspect. Upon learning the address of Dr. Erikson's home, Agent Lurk stood and as he went out of the door said, "I'm heading over there."

When his office door had closed, the sheriff nodded towards the door, "You're welcome."

"It was nice meeting you," said Detective Jaros.

"Not a very friendly man," added Detective Kalven.

"Okay, here's what you two do," said the sheriff. "Go on over to the house and offer assistance if needed, but stay in the background. I'm not going to miss him. He's Bowling Green's problem now."

While walking to their car, Detective Jaros quipped, "Who is the sheriff not going to miss, Brian Toth or the federal stiff?"

"Good question."

CHAPTER 23

"Brian, are you okay?" said Dr. Erikson.

The sound of the surgeon's voice brought him back to reality. "Yeah, you guys be quiet now. I have to make a call."

Brian turned his cell phone back on and called the nurse.

"How's he doing?"

"He's about the same Brian. No better, but no worse either."

"You have taken care of a lot of heart patients. How much more time do you think he has?"

"His body is still fairly strong, but I can't give you a timeline."

"You can't or you won't?"

"Brian, I'm praying as much as you are."

"I appreciate that Mindy. Thank you."

When Brian hung up, Dr. Bauhner said, "So you think a nurse is qualified to give a patient's prognosis?"

Before Brian could answer the question, his phone rang. When he saw who the caller was, a sad grin appeared on his face.

"Hello, Nathan, aren't you at work?"

"No, I called in and told them I wouldn't be there due to an illness in the family."

"You don't have a family, Nathan."

"You're like a brother to me Brian. I would do anything for you."

"Really, have you signed an organ donor's card?"

"Actually, I have."

"I was just kidding you Nathan. You keep your heart. I'm hoping my new celebrity status will move us up on the recipient list."

"Well, that is kind of why I called. I met this news reporter who has been following your story all day. She even interviewed me today."

"The reporter is a she? Are you doing this for me or for yourself?"

After a slight pause, Nathan said, "Both."

CHAPTER   24

After arriving at the hostage site, Agent Lurk spoke with the officers on duty there and called back to headquarters about his perspective on the situation and his intentions to remedy the problem.

"That is correct. I have ascertained that a man with a large caliber revolver holds two men hostage in the home. I'm going to assemble a SWAT team and prepare them to raid the house at an opportune time."

At the conclusion of his conversation, Agent Lurk drove over to commandeer the golf course clubhouse. Many disgruntled members voiced their displeasure at being removed from the building. A quick thinking manager moved all business transactions to the patio area. The outside bar was opened, a television was turned on and the patrons settled down to another enjoyable day of leisure.

Channel 12 Station Manager Ben Walters had been inundated all day with many calls requesting information about Ashley Ludwig. He was about to hang up on the young man asking for her phone number when the caller said, "She interviewed me this morning at McKee's Corners about Brian Toth."

"What did you say your name was?"

"Nathan Kovacs. I finally got a hold of Brian; he is near the golf course at the home of a

Dr. Noah Erikson and he has agreed to be interviewed by Ashley."

"No kidding," said Ben as his mind raced ahead. "Here's what I'd like you to do. I'll have Ashley transported to the site of that residence and can you meet her there ASAP?"

"It would be my pleasure."

The two bound doctors were getting tired of sitting in the same position. Both expressed the need to use the bathroom. Dr. Erikson told Brian, "There is a small bathroom across the hall from the game room."

Brian thought about the dilemma for a short while before he formulated a solution. After warning the doctors not to make any false moves, he placed the gun within his reach, and then retied Dr. Bauhner's ankles with just enough slack so that he would be able to shuffle his feet. Next he started to untie his wrists. When Brian got to the point where he could manage with one hand, he picked up the revolver. Finally, he removed the rope and tape that held the prisoner to his seat. Slowly, Dr. Bauhner rose and hobbled over to the bathroom. Brian followed the captive man closely there and back. Then he warily rebound him and repeated the process with Dr. Erikson. The whole procedure took quite a long time and all three men seemed relieved when it was over. Brian took his seat across from the two, sighed and said, "I hope that

you two took care of everything in the bathroom
because we won't be doing that again."

CHAPTER   25

Outside of the upscale house, the captain of the city police stood on the sidewalk and spoke with a couple of his patrolmen. They had relieved the first shift officers and were taking turns eating their supper meals. The new recruit asked the Captain, "How long do you think we'll be here, sir?"

Exercising patience with the rookie the Captain said, "We could be here all night for all I know. Right now though, you need to keep the citizens away from the house. I have requested our special unit that is familiar with hostage predicaments. When they arrive, they will first attempt to negotiate a surrender of the suspect. After that, a use of force could be utilized. The important thing is that we remain patient."

When Shannon arrived at her mother's house, she couldn't wait to tell all of her friends about the exciting events of the day. While her mother played with Megan, Shannon phoned everyone she knew and told them her story. They in turn, called their friends and the number of informed residents grew exponentially. A crowd of people had steadily grown from just a few gossipy neighbors, to a large curious crowd. Many people from the area who had been following the story all day came to see first hand, the final chapter. Some of the 'Sewer Celebrities' arrived with their numbers still displayed on their foreheads. The fun-loving neighbor from across the street stood on his front lawn with a black marker and wrote numbers on the bare foreheads of a growing line of people.

The atmosphere was festive and more than a few of the spectators were inebriated. The numbers continued to grow and when the red Channel 12 news van came rolling down the street, the mob roared. As Bob slowly weaved the vehicle through the mass, the people pounded on its sides and chanted, "Ashley, Ashley…"

Brian wanted to wait as long as possible before calling the nurse again. He knew that her report on the status of his son might very well be the stimulus to make his final decision. Part of him wanted to remain patient like maintaining a good pace in a marathon. Another part of him wanted to sprint and end the madness. He was growing weary and his thoughts drifted back to the night before when he last saw Alex.

FLASHBACK #7

Earlier in the day, before going to St. Henry's Hospital, Brian had driven to Craig's barber shop in Portage and had his year-long locks cut off. As he entered the cardiac unit, the nurse at the counter did not recognize him and stopped him.

"It's me, Mindy."

"Sorry, I didn't realize it was you, Brian. You clean up well."

"Thanks. How's he doing?"

"His appetite is good, but he sleeps a lot more."

"Would it be okay if I wake him up? I'd like to talk to him."

"Sure. He's always upbeat after your visits."

"Oh, another thing, I probably won't be able to visit tomorrow. Can I call and check up on him?"

"Yes, I am scheduled to work the next two evenings. You can call me. I'll be taking care of him."

"Thanks Mindy. We appreciate the extra effort you make."

Brian then walked down the hall and entered the low-lighted room. As he closed the door, he was pleased to see that Alex did not have a roommate that night. He quietly walked to the bed and gazed down at his sleeping son and marveled at how much Alex resembled his late wife.

"We did well, Linda"

Alex opened his eyes, blinked twice and said, "Dad, you got your hair cut."

Brian smiled. "I'm trying to change my luck."

"You don't believe in luck. You believe in hard work. I've heard you say it hundreds of times."

"I guess you were listening."

With a serious look, Alex awkwardly said, "I talked to Mom."

"I talk to Mom too, Alex."

"No, not like that. I had a dream. Mom was wearing that blue dress you bought her for your anniversary. She was smiling and very healthy and she teased me about having a girl friend, even though I don't have one at the moment."

Brian skeptically said, "Did she tell you what I should do?"

"Not exactly. She said that I should take care of you."

"I'm supposed to be taking care of you, Alexander."

"Mom said that I'm going to be okay. It's you that's causing her concern."

Brian just stared at his son. Alex added, "Anyhow, I felt like she was fading away so I hugged her and told her that I love her. When I woke up you were here."

"I'm sorry I woke you. Hey, did I tell you about the dream that I had?"

"No, tell me about it."

With devious eyes, Brian said, "In my dream you recover so quickly from the surgery that you are able to win the state crown next fall. Then you head off to college where you meet the girl of your dreams. After graduation you land a choice job and get married. You and your wife have a half dozen healthy children, all of whom are attractive and intelligent. As you live out your long lives, your family enjoys many accomplishments. They are well respected and their list of friends grows continuously."

Alex said, "I feel exhausted just hearing about it."

Brian touched his hand and was shocked at how cold he felt. When he recovered, he locked eyes with his son. "I know that I rarely say this to you, but I love you Alex. You have to know that."

"You have never needed to say that, Dad. I've always known it."

For his son's sake, Brian kept his composure and tried to sound positive. "Alex, I have a real good feeling about you getting a new heart soon."

Before drifting off to sleep, Alex said, "I believe you, Dad."

For a whole minute, Brian stood there and admired his son. "I lost you Linda, but I promise I'll save our son."

When Brian walked past the nurses' station, he didn't hear Mindy say 'good night'. His body trembled and he had a hard time walking to his car. As soon as he got into his Cavalier, he broke down and sobbed hysterically. After a few minutes though, he gained control of his emotions and wiped the tears from his face. Then he looked into his rearview mirror and said to himself, "I couldn't live without you, Alex."

CHAPTER 26

The number of policemen was increased to keep the swelling amount of spectators away from Dr. Erikson's house. The officers were amused by the antics of the locals, especially the spontaneous chants that a few jokers made up. The mood was similar to that of a ball game, particularly when the Bowling Green Bobcat cheerleaders decided to use the event for cheerleading practice.

After calling Channel 12, Nathan Kovacs drove straight to the house on the winding lane. He saw the mass of people and parked in one of the few remaining spots in the area. As he approached the crowd, he could hear music blaring from one of the decks of a neighboring home. He felt as if he was entering an outdoor concert. When Bob and Ashley drove by, he jogged behind the van as it divided the audience. When Bob finally found a parking space, Ashley checked her makeup, stepped out of the van and was welcomed by Nathan and a small entourage of gawking admirers.

Nathan looked pleased to see her, "Hello Ashley."

She smiled back at him and got down to business. "Hello, Nathan. My station manager informed me that you were able to contact Brian Toth."

"Yes, after you left me, I called his number every ten minutes until he finally answered."

"Great. What did he have to say for himself?"

"Well, besides the small talk, he was obviously concerned about locating a heart. He tends to think that not everything has been done in that area and he's hoping that all of this attention will somehow move his son to the front of the list."

Ashley slowly shook her head and said, "That sounds crazy."

The smile left Nathan's face. "You may be right, but lucky for you, you're the one he's willing to talk with."

She reached forward and grasped his forearm and said, "I didn't mean to offend you."

Nathan savored her touch and said, "Frightened and angry is a bad combination, but that is what Brian is now, Ashley."

"I'll try to avoid agitating him if you call him for me."

Nathan punched in the call to Brian and said, "Okay, Ashley, I'll see how he's doing."

Bob stood with his back to the dropping sun ready to record. Ashley said to him, "Let's not go live until after I have spoken with Brian."

"Do both of you have your cell phones with you?"

"I do," said Dr. Erikson.

"So do I, but I can't get to it tied up like this," said Dr. Bauhner.

"Well, let's see what I can do about that," said Brian. Then he went to where Dr. Bauhner sat and tied the prisoner's left wrist to his left thigh. Next he freed the doctor's right hand and repeated the procedure on Dr. Erikson.

The contented effects produced from the alcohol had long passed from Dr. Bauhner. He felt agitated and suggested, "Brian, we want to cooperate, but maybe you're not coherent due to overtraining and lack of sex for the past six months."

FLASHBACK #8

Brian would never listen to music while running because he wanted to be aware of his surroundings. Instead, he would listen to a song or two while he put on his shoes and stretched. Those tunes would be stuck in his head during the run. He had become very selective lately. His two favorites were *Hurt* by Nine Inch Nails and *Laughing* by David Crosby.

A slow steady rain had been falling since he left his house and ran shirtless down crooked Poe road towards Beaver Creek. Although Brian was not timing the run, he still concentrated on his breathing and form. After he crossed the metal frame bridge and climbed the hill with powerful strides, Brian turned right and entered the graveyard through the opened black iron gates. As he ran along the perimeter gravel road, the rain suddenly stopped.

Beyond the ravine, the cemetery had been expanded to include a secluded cul de sac, surrounded by hardwoods. So far, there were only a few graves at the new site and his late brother-in-law occupied one of them. Many times, Brian had been tempted to run over there to urinate on Ted's gravestone. However, the thought passed as he got closer because he noticed a car was parked off to the side of the narrow road, on the near side of the ravine. He decided to visit the driver of the red Corvette and followed the new road through the ravine. When he reached the far side, he walked toward the woman who held an umbrella. She wore a light sleeveless top with a tight brown leather short skirt and stood at the foot of the grave. He silently approached her from behind and when he was next to her he said, "Hello, Brenda."

She startled and he said, "You don't need the umbrella anymore."

Brenda smiled and said, "Hi Brian. I didn't notice that the rain had stopped."

He had not seen her since the holidays when her husband had killed himself. He enjoyed how much she looked like Linda. He thought, 'same

93

model, different year', but he said, "I haven't seen you for a while. I've been so occupied with Alex lately."

"I'm sorry I haven't visited him. How's he doing?"

"They just put him on the thirty day waiting list, so he'll receive a transplant just as soon as a heart becomes available."

She thought about what had happened to her sister a half a year earlier and wasn't sure what to say to him next.

Brian broke the awkward silence and said, "So what have you been up to?"

She sighed and said, "Since Ted's death, I only have left the house to go grocery shopping and sometimes to attend church. Most days I come here for a visit."

Brian said nothing and Brenda suspected that was because he never really accepted her late husband's abrasive personality. She had not had a heart to heart talk with anyone in years and desperately wanted answers to many questions. Finally she said, "I feel so confused, Brian. My husband is gone. I have no children and I'm not sure what I should do next."

Brian gave her a look of disbelief. "Brenda, you're still young. And now that you are free, you can do anything you want. I'm sure that over the past years, you have dreamed about being in a different situation. You're smart. You could go back to school and be whatever you want to be."

"Well, there's always that option, but what do you mean about me wanting to change my circumstance?"

"Brenda, your confidence was never that high and your husband liked to keep you down, so I assumed that you wanted to change that."

Her conditioned response was to defend the man buried six feet down. "He wasn't that bad to me. I thought he was happy and I guess I'll never know why he took his own life. The note that he left for me didn't explain much."

Brian's curiosity got the best of him. "What did the note say?"

A tear rolled down her cheek and she said, "He said that he 'couldn't live like this anymore' and I don't know what he meant by that. I didn't change anything that I was doing."

"Did you notice any changes in him?"

"Many. He became lazy, depressed and was gaining weight. Plus, he no longer had any interest in having sex with me."

She blushed and covered her mouth with her hand, shocked that she had offered such personal information.

Brian hesitated then said, "Brenda, you deserved better. I'd be lying if I said I missed him."

Visibly offended she said, "You're just like everyone else. I know he wasn't perfect. He had some minor faults. Since Ted's death, a lot of people have suggested that he had done so many bad things, but nobody has offered any proof."

Brian wanted to spill his guts to her, but doubted that she would believe him. Instead he said, "You've only made one mistake in your life Brenda, but now it's been erased."

She slapped him across the face and it unleashed the truth from him. "Alright, you want proof? I'll give you some, but I doubt that you're willing to accept the truth! "

As Brenda stood seething on the grave, Brian repeated the account that Linda had told him while on her deathbed. When he concluded the rape story, Brian noticed that she was nodding, finally resigned to the facts.

Without speaking, she tossed the umbrella and her purse off to the side and with both hands, pulled the hem of her skirt up to her breasts. After watching Brian's physical reaction, she removed her white panties, turned around, took two steps and bent over, grasping the grey granite headstone for balance. Brian didn't hesitate. Instead, he quickly took off his running shorts and got behind her. As he unclasped her bra and groped her hard nipples, she reached back through her legs and inserted his erection into herself. With unbridled enthusiasm, they savored each thrust until a near synchronized climax was reached. Brian thought to himself, if Ted's eyes are open, he has one heck of a view.

When they uncoupled, Brian watched as the fluid dripped off of him onto the newly planted grass as Brenda retrieved her purse. After she wiped herself with a tissue, she handed one to Brian. He cleaned himself off and then they both got dressed. Feeling vindicated, Brenda broke the silence, and said, "I'm never coming back here again."

They left the soiled tissues fluttering on the grave and walked together, slowly through the ravine, back to her car. She kissed Brian on the cheek, got into her car and started the engine. Before driving away, she lowered the window and with a twinkle in her eye said, "That has to be the ultimate revenge."

Brian watched the sports car exit the cemetery and before continuing his run said, "Brenda, you can read my mind."

CHAPTER 27

The audio surveillance van of the Bowling Green Special Unit drove on the golf cart path until it arrived at the back of the Erikson home. The backyard and golf course had been kept clear of spectators by an increasing number of police officers. Without the noise of the mob out front, the hostage team focused their receiver on the basement windows. The vibrations on the glass from the sounds inside the home were transmitted to the equipment that took up half of the space of the crowded van. The sound waves were amplified and noise was filtered out. The resulting enhanced signals were fed into a computer and a program was used that would try to determine what was being said. In optimum situations, whole conversations could be heard, but so far only a few words were being picked up. The words would appear on the screen only when the computer was certain of what they were. Technicians listened in using headsets and recorded everything. By making adjustments, they were able to increase the collection of words. When a large enough vocabulary was learned, the computer could pick up fractions of words and determine what they were, much like a hearing impaired person reading lips. Eventually complete sentences were available and at that point, the officer in charge of the Special Unit informed the captain of their progress.

"Captain, we're able to decipher most of what is being said at this point."

"Would it help if we quieted the crowd?"

"I don't believe so, sir. The computer has locked in on their voices and is now able to ignore all of the other sounds."

"I wish I could do that. Are they still in the basement?"

"From the conversations thus far, we believe that all three of them are still in the same room together and the two hostages are still bound. We aren't able to confirm the exact arrangement of the men in the room. They may or may not be situated as Mrs. Erikson described earlier."

"Does the suspect seem agitated or irrational?"

"No, he is pretty calm and soft spoken. For the most part, the atmosphere is relaxed, but I believe that one of the hostages is becoming a little testy."

"I would like to contact Mr. Toth as soon as possible. The federal agent is gung-ho about raiding the place, but I would rather try negotiations first."

"Let us listen in a while longer and see what develops. The more information we gather, the easier your decision will be."

"Okay, but get ahold of me fast if there is any hint of violence."

"Are you on something, because you seem to fade in and out?"

Brian pointed the handgun at the offensive man and said, "Dr. Bauhner, keep annoying me and you'll make my decision easy."

The color left the face of the hostage and as he cringed in his seat he said, "Please don't shoot me. I'm not ready to die yet."

"Death is rarely convenient."

The doctors watched as Brian lowered the gun and a visible change came over him. By slowly inhaling a few deep breathes of air, a noticeable calm reclaimed the tormented man. Then he said, "Okay. Now I want both of you to think of any connections that you might have, any favor that is owed to you or whatever avenue has not been tried yet to locate a heart."

Still perspiring, Dr. Bauhner immediately began sorting through the numbers on his cell phone with his thumb. Dr. Erikson, however, sat still and said, "That's not how it works. It's a waiting game, Brian. Three thousand people are in line for a heart, but the process is in motion and when a heart becomes available, we will perform the operation. Until then, we can only wait and pray."

This time, Brian pointed the gun at Dr. Erikson and said, "I have learned a great deal about the organ donor program this past year. You two, not only taught me about the details of the process, but you also inadvertently shared personal information about yourselves. Most important to me is the fact that both of you are organ donor card carriers who have the same genetic similarities as my family."

Dr. Erikson startled when Brian's cell phone rang and he immediately began calling his medical colleagues looking for a solution to his dilemma. Brian answered his phone.

"Hey, Nathan, where are you?"

"Hi Brian, I'm just down the street from where you're at and I have the newswoman Ashley Ludwig with me."

"What do you think of her?"

Nathan looked at Ashley and said, "She's beautiful Brian, and smart, though not necessarily in that order. I'm going to put her on the phone now."

"Before you do that Nathan, tell me what is going on outside of this house."

"There are gobs of people. It's kind of like a parade out here."

"What are the police doing?"

"It looks like they have the house surrounded and are keeping everyone else away from it."

"After I talk with your girlfriend, maybe you could walk down there and keep an eye on the police for me."

"Sure, Brian. Good luck. Here's Ashley."

Nathan handed her the phone. "Thanks, Nathan. Mr. Toth, this is Ashley Ludwig with Channel 12 News."

Brian took a moment to listen to the two captive doctors then returned his attention to his phone and said, "Ashley, you can call me Brian."

"Brian, I have been covering your story all day. Starting with the incident in Potterville, then to St. Henry's where I was able to speak with your victims as they left the hospital. Oh, by the way, they all forgive you except for the guy named Don."

"Don is still a jerk."

"Forgiveness is usually a two way street Brian, are you able to forgive?"

"I find it difficult in some cases, but I don't believe that I'm any different than most people. We all struggle with the demons of our past."

"You know that I have interviewed Nathan. But I also spoke with Martha McKee about you."

"Martha is a good woman. I'm sure whatever she said about me is the honest truth."

"She said that you are family."

Brian sighed and said, "I'm going to miss her."

"You have had quite the day so far. What do you plan to do next?"

"I believe the search for a heart will end in this room, one way or another."

Ashley was taken aback by the statement and said, "Brian, you're not suggesting sacrificing a good man for the sake of your son, are you?"

Growing impatient, Brian said, "I am ready to do whatever it takes to save Alex."

Flabbergasted, Ashley said, "You're not being very rational, Brian. First the revenge and now this. Are you playing God, is that it?"

Before turning off his phone, Brian shouted, "God gave up his only son, but I will not!"

CHAPTER 28

Ashley looked worried as she handed the phone back to Nathan. "I'm sorry, I screwed up. He got mad and hung up on me. That wasn't the way I wanted it to go."

Nathan wanted to tell her that everything was okay, but it wasn't okay. So instead he said, "You have some people here who want to talk to you."

As Nathan went to spy on the police, Ashley was approached by representatives from one national and two local television stations. The two local news reporters only wanted to pump her for new information for their own broadcasts. However, the big name network wanted to air Ashley's newscast nationwide. She felt honored but nervous and after an update and pep talk from Ben Walters, agreed with the arrangement.

With the horde of noisy people in the background, she spoke with confidence at the camera. "Good evening, this is Ashley Ludwig reporting to you from the home of Dr. Noah Erikson here in Bowling Green, Ohio. Today has been a day of contradictions. If you have been following the accounts of suspect Brian Toth, you witnessed acts of revenge in the form of abduction and punishment followed by forgiveness. Currently another inconsistency in Mr. Toth's behavior is being played out at the home of one of the cardiac surgeons from St. Henry's hospital. Alexander Toth, the son of Brian, is lying in a bed at that hospital awaiting a heart transplant. At the same time, Brian Toth is holding hostage the two surgeons who will probably perform the operation, once an organ becomes available. Just a few minutes ago, I spoke with the suspect via cell phone. Our conversation was short lived as Mr. Toth grew increasingly agitated with my questions and I got the sense that the lives of the two men, who could save Alex, are in jeopardy…"

Trying to be inconspicuous, Nathan worked his way through the commotion and got within earshot of a small group of Bowling Green's finest. A rookie officer in the group was impressed with the entertainment provided by the spectators and when he shared his thoughts with some of the veterans, one of them said with a straight face, "This is nothing. You should have been in Perrysburg last weekend for the Gay Pride parade. They had free bareback llama rides."

"Really?" said the young officer.

They all had a good laugh at the rookie's expense. The Captain walked over to them and the mood became somber. One of the older officers said, "Any news, Captain?"

"That's what I came to tell you. The Special Unit has informed me that the suspect is beginning to unravel. They have intercepted the phone conversations of all three of the men and it has been decided to appease the suspect by informing him that a suitable donor has been found. When he takes the bait, we will arrest him and free the hostages. Also, I have just gotten off of the phone with Federal Agent Lurk. He has agreed with my plan, but if it fails, he wants to raid the home immediately.

Martin Jaros joined the group of officers and caught the tail end of the Captain's news. The Captain acknowledged him with a nod but continued his talk with the officers.

"We are concerned about a friend of the suspect who has made phone contact with him recently. The man's name is Nathan Kovacs. We don't have a good description of him yet, but I don't want him tipping off the suspect..."

Detective Jaros spoke up, "Captain, I know what Nathan Kovacs looks like. He was with Ashley before she did her broadcast. In fact, he was standing right in back of you a few seconds ago."

All of the officers turned to look in that direction and Detective Jaros pointed and said, "That's him there with the Cleveland Brown's jersey on, heading away from us."

When Nathan had overheard the plan, he quickly walked away from the police trying to get lost into the crowd. He tried to contact Brian, but there was no answer so he attempted to leave a message. A short time later he was tackled from behind by two of the officers. As one of them knelt on his neck, the other handcuffed him. They pulled him to his feet and rushed him to the nearest cruiser as the shocked onlookers got out of the way.

CHAPTER 29

Shannon Erikson stayed at her mother's house with Megan as long as she could stand it. All of her life she had been the center of attention and after viewing the latest report on the national network, she felt the need to make an appearance. After a quick rinse in the shower, she tried on her latest outfit recently purchased from Annie's boutique in West Toledo. A self-evaluation in front of the full-length mirror, verified that the blouse with the plunging neckline and the high-waisted tight black slacks, accentuated her firm figure. After locating her Kate Spade bag, she put on a new pair of black pumps with the red soles and heels and grabbed the matching designer purse. Satisfied, she gave a fast farewell to her mother and daughter and drove off in the SUV to Candy Land Lane. Instead of driving through the crowd, she decided to park her vehicle on the street and make her entrance on foot. As the doctor's wife entered the fringe of spectators, she couldn't help but notice one of the young men. Before she could slip by him, he said, "Good evening, Mrs. Erikson."

Shannon thought to herself, 'I really should go to confession one of these days'. But, she said, "Hello, Father Matt. What brings you out to our neighborhood?"

"Curiosity for one thing, but mainly I'm attempting to organize a prayer group that hopefully will bring about a peaceful outcome."

"How's that going so far, Father?"

The priest scanned the many surrounding people who wore numbers on their foreheads and said, "I haven't been very successful yet. As you can see, it's kind of like a perverse version of Ash Wednesday here."

"I can see why you might feel that way. Well, I want to take a closer look Father, so I'll see you later."

"Maybe on Sunday?"

When Shannon walked away, Father Matt was the only man in the area who averted his eyes.

From a cruiser headed back toward the Bowling Green city jail, an officer who had arrested Nathan was receiving instructions from the captain.

"Don't book him yet. Just place him in a holding cell. This is only a precaution at the time. We can't have him alerting the suspect."

Before calling the chief to discuss his plan, the captain ordered his men to clear the street of all of the pedestrians.

"Get all of these people off of the roadway. Either keep them across the street or two houses away from this one. Only make arrests if absolutely necessary. I want this lane open for the SWAT team and any emergency vehicles that we request. Got it? Okay, get it done."

    With the revolver resting on his lap, Brian slouched in his chair across from the two doctors. After listening to their phone conversations, it became apparent to him that neither surgeon was having any luck locating a heart donor. He knew that this part of the plan was probably foolish, but he had to get through it before he could justify the next step. Finally, when he couldn't take it anymore he said, "Dr. Bauhner, you keep trying. Dr. Erikson, I want you to call the hospital. Have them round up your team and make preparations for surgery. Get them to prep the patient and send an organ transport vehicle over here. Then tell me when all is ready."

CHAPTER   30

While his officers were convincing the spectators to clear the street and the area near the doctor's home, the captain walked around the house to the audio surveillance van. He was beginning to experience that familiar feeling he had at every confrontation. The pressure was building and although he didn't have as short of a fuse as Agent Lurk, he seemed a bit on edge as he opened the van door to speak with the audio surveillance leader.

"Give me an update."

The officer without the headset said, "I was just about to contact you. The suspect is forcing the two surgeons to use any clout that they have to try and locate a heart for his son. It doesn't sound like they are having any success on their cell phones. There is an implied threat that one of the doctors could be used as a donor. Mr. Toth has gone so far as to order Dr. Erikson to make all arrangements for the operation."

"Thank you. Let me know if the threat escalates."

After the captain closed the van door he called the chief and relayed the information to him. Then he added, "I'm going to go ahead and feed the suspect the fabricated story through one of the doctors."

The Chief agreed and said, "Okay. I've thought about the plan and it might fool the suspect into coming out of the house. I think that you should use Dr. Bauhner to deliver the message. Unlike Dr. Erikson, Richard has no family and has a reputation as a playboy, so he's used to lying."

"Good point."

The captain then contacted Agent Lurk who was chomping at the bit to move his SWAT team.

"Alright Lurk, were going to contact the suspect and try to talk him out of the house. If that doesn't work then we'll resort to using the SWAT team."

"We should have raided the house a long time ago, captain. This case would have been wrapped up by now."

The captain's ire grew, but couldn't be detected in his voice when he said, "Bring your team over here and stage them in the neighbor's front yard. If we can't talk the suspect out of there, then he's all yours."

CHAPTER 31

Fear had overcome the ridiculous feeling that Dr. Bauhner initially had when he began calling colleagues. All attempts to locate a donor heart were in vain and just when the surgeon had run out of hospitals to contact, he received a call.

"Dr. Bauhner, don't overreact. Yes or no, can Mr. Toth hear my voice?"

"No."

"This is the captain of the Bowling Green Police Department, but you can call me Dr. Hashanti from Ann Arbor."

"Okay."

"Don't worry, if Mr. Toth takes the phone from you, I will play the part and cover for you. If he calls this number back or contacts Dr. Hashanti, then that will be handled also."

"Good."

"We have been listening to what is going on in there and have decided to tell the suspect what he wants to hear. As far as you know this story could be true, so act that way. Be optimistic. Here's the deal. Again, my name is Dr. Hashanti from Ann Arbor. We have never met. A donor heart has been located west of Detroit in the form of an auto fatality of a 20-year-old white male college student and is headed your way in a helicopter. Don't over sell it. Just feed him the details that he craves and let him take the bait. Do you feel confident?"

"Yes."

"Then give him a quick look, act thrilled, then focus on this conversation."

Dr. Bauhner met Brian's gaze, sat up straight and began nodding before he said, "Great, give me the details."

"Dr. Hashanti from Ann Arbor, 20 year old student, helicopter. Have you gained his attention?"

"Yes. Excellent."

"The heart will arrive at St. Henry's in thirty minutes."

"Wonderful!"

"We're confident that this will succeed and remember we are listening, but as a precaution, if you say that you 'need to feed your dog,' we will come in. Alright, after you hang up, give him the details, but don't push it."

After the street was cleared, the crowd seemed to settle down like the halftime at a football game. The atmosphere of the spectators had abated to the point that the police thought that the party was over and that most of the people would soon leave the area. Unfortunately, just as the crowd began to dwindle, a large black SUV followed by a dark truck van rumbled down the street narrowly missing a jaywalker. When the two vehicles came to a stop in the neighbor's driveway, a toilet paper streamer sailed towards them from across the street. As Agent Lurk exited the SUV he was nearly struck in the head with a nerf football. The crowd roared with laughter and the party had new life. The black cladded SWAT team poured out of the truck van and was met with a chorus of boos. They unloaded their gear on the neighbor's front lawn and then began to load their weapons.

CHAPTER 32

When Ashley heard that Nathan had been arrested, she felt partially responsible. As she and Bob had worked their way through the mass of people, they asked if anyone had seen what had happened to Nathan. One man said that the arrest had occurred at the other end of the group near the priest, but before the news crew could reach the clergyman, there was a commotion nearby.

Without ever breaking stride, Shannon strutted down the sidewalk towards her home. The crowd parted as it sensed her aura. She left in her wake, a tide of inquisitive gawkers. Despite herself, Ashley said, "Who is that?"

Without taking his eyes off of the doctor's wife, a middle aged neighbor said, "That's Mrs. Erikson, the doctor's wife."

Ashley hustled toward the striking figure and shouted for the woman to stop, but Shannon ignored her, until she saw the camera.

Brian had been listening intently to Dr. Bauhner when Dr. Erikson said, "Alright Brian, I did everything you said to do. The surgical team is assembling, the patient is being prepped and a rescue squad has been dispatched to this location."

Without taking his eyes off of Dr. Bauhner, Brian said, "Thank you Dr. Erikson. Dr. Bauhner, what do you have for me?"

Dr. Bauhner put on his happy face and said, "I just received a call from a Dr. Hashanti in Ann Arbor. He informed me that a donor heart became available this past hour from an automobile accident somewhere outside of Detroit."

The lying doctor paused for the gunman to digest the good news. "The healthy heart was extracted and is heading to St. Henry's in a helicopter."

"Who was the donor?"

"Well, I don't know his name, but he was a white, twenty-year-old male college student."

Brian fought the urge to be jubilant. His resting heart rate of 37 beats per minute made his body visibly shudder. For a very short time, he felt euphoric, but he became skeptical when he saw the anxious look in Dr. Bauhner's eyes.

The two men studied each other. Brian responded, "I wish I could be certain."

Immediately regretting his choice of words, Dr. Bauhner said, "What do you have to lose?"

CHAPTER 33

"Mrs. Erikson, please stop," Ashley shouted.

Shannon tried not to smile when she halted and faced the camera. The people nearby gave them room to operate.

"I'd like to ask you a few questions if I could."

As Bob aimed his camera, Shannon held her shoulders back and said, "Sure, why not?"

"This must be a very difficult day for you with your husband and his partner being held hostage. I empathize with you and appreciate any amount of information you can offer us."

Shannon shrugged and said, "No problem."

The newswoman appeared somber as she faced the camera and said, "This is Ashley Ludwig and with me now is the courageous wife of Dr. Erikson."

She then turned toward Shannon. "I don't know if it has been made public yet, but I understand that you were also a hostage this morning."

"That is correct. I was the one who answered the door when Brian first appeared on our doorstep."

"That must have been very frightening for you."

"It was at first, but eventually I could tell that he wasn't going to hurt anyone. I mean, he let me go so that I could pick up my daughter from school."

"So in your opinion, you believe that Mr. Toth is relatively harmless?"

"I think everything is going to be okay."

Before Ashley could ask another question, a commotion near the doctor's house distracted them and Shannon's curiosity drew her to it. By the time Shannon had pushed her way to the edge of the police line the crowd was chanting, "Don't shoot, don't shoot..." As she introduced herself to the rookie cop, two nearby policemen came over to help the young officer protect her.

"They're not going to raid my home are they?"

The young cop said, "No ma'am. The presence of the SWAT team is only a safeguard. No one is going to get hurt."

"Then why is that here?" Shannon pointed to the ambulance parking in front of her home.

CHAPTER   34

Agent Lurk went over the plan with the SWAT team in the front yard and told them to be ready for his order. Then he walked around to the backyard to meet with the police captain. At the van, the head audio surveillance officer switched the sound from his head phones to the speakers and adjusted the sound just loud enough so that the captain and Agent Lurk could hear the conversations taking place in the basement.

"Did you ask me what I think only to tell me what you think?"

The phony smile left Dr. Bauhner's face. "No Brian, I'm only relaying the information. Heck, if we leave now we can begin operating in an hour."

Dr. Erikson nodded in agreement as Brian considered his next course of action. Finally, he said, "Before I agree, I need to make one last phone call."

As the sun sat over the plush golf course, the decision makers huddled around the rear of the van and anxiously awaited Brian's pronouncement. In the front yard the SWAT team took on the appearance of a visiting football team awaiting the kickoff. As the men in black calmly stretched out, the crowd jeered them. Lighted candles began appearing around where the priest stood and Ashley recognized some of the morning 'Sewer Celebrities' in attendance.

Brian had mixed feelings about placing the call, but he knew that soon his dilemma would be resolved. His palms were sweaty and as he held the .44 in his right hand, he used his left to turn his phone back on and called the hospital.

After the third ring, Mindy answered her phone and said, "Hello Brian, I've been dreading this call".

"Me too. How's he doing?"

"Brian, I could lose my job for this."

"I'm sorry, Mindy, but I have to know."

Mindy hesitated then blurted out, "They wanted me to tell you that Alex's vital signs are improving, but the truth is, his color looks bad and his breathing is labored."

"Could I talk to him?"

"I could put the phone up to his ear and he might hear you, but I doubt that he would speak with you. I'm sorry, Brian. I have to hang up now. Someone is coming."

In the backyard Agent Lurk gave the captain a venomous look and said, "I thought you had everything covered?"

"Hang on, we may still be alright."

As the police held back the crowd on one side of the house, they continued to shout, "Don't shoot." When the group on the other side of the house began chanting Brian's name, the two dueling cheers joined to create the chant, "Don't shoot Brian, Don't shoot…"

Brian wiped his brow with the back of his hand and said, "I have to make a decision now."

The two hostages looked at him with hopeful eyes and Dr. Erikson asked, "What did the nurse tell you?"

"She inferred that surgery couldn't wait any longer."

Dr. Bauhner said, "We're ready if you are."

Brian nodded slightly. "Before I release the two of you, let me tell you about plan B."

Looking down at the loaded revolver in his hand he continued. "If a heart couldn't be located today, one of you was going to donate yours. You're both donor card carrying perfect candidates.

So tell me, if I had gone with plan B, whose heart should I have chosen?"

Both surgeons sensed a trap, but Dr. Bauhner spoke up first. "I sometimes smoke cigars, but Noah runs every day."

Dr. Erikson looked aghast and said, "Richard, you told me just the other day that you rode your bike on the Slippery Elm trail all the way to North Baltimore and back. You bragged to me that you made the trip in record time!"

Brian held out his left hand requesting silence and assumed a contemplative posture. When he lowered his hand he noticed that he had a message on his phone.

Agent Lurk gave the police captain a disgusted look and radioed the lead man of the SWAT team and said, "All three are still in the game room. Have your guys unlock the front door and disable the security system. Move the team up close, but don't go in the house unless I give the order."

CHAPTER   35

Brian pressed a button with his thumb and when he saw that the message was from Nathan, he put the phone to his ear and listened to it. The two doctors looked on with concern as Brian's body became tense, his face contorted with anger and he mumbled, "Liars."

When Dr. Bauhner looked away, Dr. Erikson said, "What's wrong?"

Brian inhaled deeply until his hands stopped shaking. He hit the button for speakerphone and replayed the message from Nathan. "Brian, I remembered what you said about loyalty. So I have to tell you, it's a hoax. There is no donor. The police are lying…"

The rest of the unintelligible message was followed by scuffle sounds then the phone went dead.

Brian slowly shook his head. "Dr. Bauhner, look at me."

Both doctors looked worried and Brian said, "You disappoint me. Once again, you gave me hope and then took it away."

With tears in his eyes, Brian looked up and said, "It is finished."

Then he gripped the revolver with both hands, stepped forward and aimed the gun at the head of Dr. Bauhner and said to him, "If I don't shoot you, will you perform the operation?"

Dr. Bauhner shrank in his seat and said, "Yes, I have to feed my dog, but yes, I promise I will!"

Brian then pointed the gun at Dr. Erikson's head and made the same offer. "How about you. If I spare your life, do you also promise to perform the transplant?"

With wide eyes, Dr. Erikson said, "I want to live. Yes, I will save your son."

At the audio surveillance van, all eyes were on the captain when he said, "Oh no. I think he's going to do it."

"No Kidding." Agent Lurk sarcastically said before shouting into his radio, "Go, go, go!"

As both doctors looked on in horror, Brian cocked the gun and pointed it at the head of Dr. Erikson. When that surgeon closed his eyes, Brian then aimed the barrel between the eyes of Dr. Bauhner. After what must have seemed like an eternity, Brian pointed the gun at his own temple and pulled the trigger.

CHAPTER 36

After the solo shot, the SWAT team crashed through the game room door. The two doctors looked as if they had just finished riding the Top Thrill Dragster roller coaster at Cedar Point Amusement Park. Brian's body lay twitching on the carpeted floor next to the air hockey game, which was covered in blood, short strands of hair and bone chips.

Disappointed that the suspect had done their job for them, the SWAT team retreated to the large living room where a sympathetic Agent Lurk consoled them. The Bowling Green police captain brushed past them with a couple of officers and descended the stairs leading to the game room. He had his men unbind the two captives and then said to the doctors, "I'll have the paramedics take you to the hospital for treatment."

Dr. Erikson said, "There's no time for that. Have them take the body to St. Henry's and prep it for surgery in the operating room next to that of the recipient."

Dr. Bauhner said, "You can't be serious, Noah. After everything we've been through today..."

"Richard, it's no longer about you or me or Brian. It's only about Alex now."

With great urgency, the paramedics lifted the body dressed in the brown uniform and placed it onto a stretcher. They covered it with a sheet and carried it up the stairs, through the house and out the front door. The apprehensive onlookers became silent and as the group exited the home, Shannon cried out, "Richard!"

Both doctors pretended not to hear her. The paramedics secured the stretcher in the rescue squad and the surgeons accompanied them. As the vehicle began the short drive to St. Henry's, Dr. Bauhner said to his partner, "Do I still get the sword?"

Dr. Erikson said, "We'll have to talk about it later. We'll have to talk about many things, Richard."

Soon after the sirens of the departed rescue squad diminished, Agent Lurk and the SWAT team got into their vehicles and also left the scene along with the audio surveillance van and much of the police force. Nathan Kovacs was released from the holding cell and given a ride back to his car by one of the patrolmen. The shameful crowd dwindled away into the darkness while Ashley spoke with Margaret Shultz, Detective Martin Jaros and Father Matt. After the trio had given her their impressions of the day's events, she left them and walked with the cameraman to the front of the Erikson home and said, "Bob, let's do one more report and then head back to the station."

The cameraman said, "You look exhausted Ashley. Wouldn't you rather take a break and get some supper first?"

"No, I want to finish this while it's still fresh in my head. Besides, after what I've witnessed today, I've never felt more alive."

Facing the camera, she turned her back to the house and said, "This is Ashley Ludwig of Channel 12 News with my final report today on the life of Brian Toth. A short while ago, the search for a donor heart for Alexander Toth ended when one became available. When all other options were exhausted and with time running out, Brian Toth the former runner, husband and father, made the ultimate sacrifice. His body was quickly rushed to St. Henry's Hospital where the heart transplant will take place.

I spoke with Father Matt of St. Louis here in Bowling Green and he informed me of the Church's stance on suicide. According to the priest, 'A man who takes his own life cannot make it into heaven'. I hope and pray that God can relate to the circumstances and will make an exception so that Brian will find redemption with his wife Linda.

The pressure is now on the two doctors who were held hostage for most of the day by the victim. If these weary surgeons can successfully transplant the good heart from the father into the son, the greatest tragedy will be averted. Then the only remaining question is: What will Alexander's mental state be when he learns the identity of the donor?"

AFTERWORD

On the first Saturday in November, an unusually large crowd filled the stands at Scioto Downs in Columbus Ohio for the annual high school cross-country state championship. Although the remaining leaves on the trees were bright with autumn colors, the weather and atmosphere surrounding the event felt like springtime. With much trepidation, newswoman Ashley Ludwig stood with cameraman Bob near the finish line. She had turned down offers from big city news stations to remain at home in Grand Rapids. At her side was Nathan Kovacs who wouldn't want to be anywhere else. In the stands sat a woman who recently resumed using her maiden name. Brenda Fejes, six months pregnant with the child she thought she could never have, beamed with pride.

A hush fell over the record number of spectators and as the starter fired his pistol into the air, Alexander Toth surged to the lead and the miracle continued.

Comeuppance Eve

CHAPTER   1

Having completed his chores for the day, Brian hurried back to his house to clean up. When Father Matt had seen him last week during a hospital visit with his son Alex, Brian had agreed to another counseling session at the church. The feeding and watering of the ten captives, now in his care, took longer than he had planned for, but he still wanted to shower and change before his therapy appointment. He made good time driving into town and a parking place across from the front of the church became available just as he arrived. As he jogged up the steps near the stone lion heads, he reached for the handle of the large, arched wooden door. But when he stepped into the dark vestibule, he realized his mistake. He was at the wrong location. It was a simple error that could be easily fixed, but Brian reminded himself to stay focused. He had set in motion a process that he could no longer back away from.

Despite being very busy, young Father Matt made time for Brian Toth to discuss his dismal circumstances. To do so, the priest had canceled his religion class with the fourth graders at St. Louis parish. This time for privacy reasons, Brian met the trained counselor at his modest home across the street from the vintage tan brick church with the red tiled roof. In the small living room the clergyman had Brian sit on the newer upholstered chair while he sat across the room in the worn recliner. Brian always marveled at how tall Father Matt was. At six feet seven inches and fresh out of the seminary, he would have had a future as a basketball player instead of a priest, had he not been so clumsy. The presence of the large man and the dark painted walls made the room seem smaller than it was. Its only adornment was a large painting of a guardian angel, either St. Michael or St. Gabriel. Brian couldn't be sure and decided not to ask.

Not one to beat around the bush, Father Matt began with a pointed question, "Brian, do you pray everyday?"

"Of course I do, but I'm not so sure it does any good."

"Give me an example of what you say when you pray."

"I say the normal prayers, but usually, I ask for things. Like forgiveness, if any of this is my fault. I ask for favors. Life shouldn't have to be so tough all the time. And, I ask for miracles, which may or may not be real. Sometimes I get so angry that I stop asking and start demanding. I find myself shouting at the sky, what do you want from me? Where are you God? Show yourself!"

Father Matt took a deep breath then said, "Brian, you have the right to be angry, but I'm not so sure you should blame God for all of your troubles."

"I don't blame Him for everything, but isn't God all powerful and all knowing? Isn't He the One who decides all things? Why is there so much suffering in the world?"

Father Matt took a moment to ponder the question then said, "God doesn't cause the pain, the sin of mankind does."

Brian raised his voice, "So, what do I have to do to end this misery?"

Father Matt decided to change the direction of the conversation. "Have you been getting enough sleep lately?"

"I try, but a lot of times I find myself laying in bed wondering how I got in this predicament. I imagine all of the people who I hold accountable and I want to hurt them."

"Each time we meet you seem less rational."

Brian frowned and said, "Okay, so then tell me again the many logical ways to relieve the stress."

"Well, there are forgiveness, prayer and relaxation techniques."

"You forgot revenge. I have tried all of your other suggestions and they work somewhat, but the thought of comeuppance gives me, by far, the most relief and satisfaction."

Father Matt leaned forward and said, "Revenge is a very dangerous concept and should be left for God to decide."

"I'm tired of waiting for the Supreme Intervention. Do I have to wait my entire life to see the good people get rewarded and the wicked punished?"

Father Matt sighed, "You may have to wait that long. No one has a definite answer, but the important thing is that you believe in the power of prayer and stay faithful. If you do that, good things will happen."

"I don't know how much faith I have left. I'm not sure what to believe anymore. No one can definitely prove to me, one way or another, that God even exists. But, I still have great hope. I hope there is a Heaven and Hell and I hope everyone gets what he or she deserves."

"So do I Brian."

Father Matt felt like he was running out of ideas to help Brian. Besides showing compassion and praying for his troubles, he wondered if the counseling sessions were doing any good, but he pushed on, "I haven't seen you at confession in a while. You know you can't be close to God with an unclean soul. I could share with you the Sacrament of Confession right here if you'd like."

Brian shook his head and said, "No, God already knows which sins I'm sorry for. With all due respect, I don't think I need to share them with you to be forgiven."

"The Sacraments are the regulations of the Church. These rules are in place to show the people how to behave."

"Sounds like they're used to control people."

"Yes, but in a good way. They are enacted to keep people close to God and away from sin."

"Father, are there any sins that can't be forgiven?"

"No, if a person is truly remorseful and asks for forgiveness, it shall be granted."

"Even mortal sins like murder and suicide?"

"God can forgive all sins no matter how bad, though I'm a little concerned about why you asked that question."

"I guess I just want to know where I stand compared to real bad people. That's all."

"Well, we obviously think differently."

Brian pointed at the priest and said, "You hit the nail on the head there, Father. You're a theologian and as such, you draw a conclusion and then seek evidence to prove it. I, on the other hand, have a scientific mind. Which means, I gather information and then form a conclusion from the data."

This statement angered the priest but he tried not to show it. "Wow, that's deep. So Brian, since you're being philosophical, why don't you tell me what you expect from this life."

"I want three things. I want to thank anyone who has ever helped me. I want a chance to say I'm sorry to anyone who deserves an apology. And, I want to die before my son does."

At that, Father Matt looked at his watch and said, "Those are all reasonable goals and expectations. So we'll discuss this further the next time we meet. Our time is up for today, but before you go, tell me how Alex is doing."

Before answering the question, Brian stared at the picture of the angel and then reluctantly looked at the priest and said, "I'm worried to death about him. I don't know what else I can do anymore. But, like I said, I still have hope and I hope everyone else is doing all they can to save him."

Father Matt walked Brian to the door, shook his hand, watched him walk away and worried about him.

CHAPTER 2

Brian started his car and turned right on Clough Street. A couple of blocks later, he turned left and headed south out of Bowling Green. Along the way, he thought about the enjoyment he got from the simple things in life, like driving his worn blue Cavalier. He realized that soon many, if not all of his freedoms, would be taken away from him and it also dawned on him that Father Matt was probably right. He had become less and less rational during the past couple of weeks. The lack of sleep and stress brought on from Alex's declining health had twisted Brian's normally logical mind. He had come to believe that obtaining a celebrity status would afford him things that normal people rarely had access to. He had witnessed star athletes, movie stars and politicians receive preferential treatment even when it came to organ transplants. Heck, Mickey Mantle got a new liver and a sixty-five year old politician received a replacement heart. It seemed as if the chosen few were catered to at the expense of the rest of the pawns. Using twisted logic, Brian convinced himself that he could elevate his ranking by becoming a celebrity even if it was made possible through illegal methods. He felt that if he could succeed at drawing attention to the plight of his son, a heart transplant for Alex would become a priority. But, now in a moment of clarity, Brian saw how insane his plan was and sank further into depression. He knew it would be best to leave the fate of his son's life in the Hands of God and the medical system, but it was too late for that now.

The sight of recently planted farm fields gradually changed into a neighborhood of old smaller houses. Brian looked at himself in the rearview mirror and admired his shoulder length hair one last time. In five minutes, he reached the small town of Portage. The town consisted of a quarry and a few rundown businesses. One of them, a small red brick building, was where Brian pulled into and parked in the gravel lot behind Craig's barbershop. There were five other vehicles already there and Brian knew he would have a wait before his haircut transformation. When he walked through the back door, he was greeted with stares from four older, short-haired men sitting in the waiting chairs. The youngest of the group, a partially bald guy who had been talking loudly in the small shop, gave Brian the stink eye. According to the patch on his shirt, his name was Jack. The other gray-haired gentlemen seemed less judgmental. The barber was the only one who appeared to be glad to see him. Craig had built his shop fifty years earlier and radiated enthusiasm about his occupation and life in general. He smiled at the sight of the younger client and said, "Wow, Brian Toth, it's been a couple of years since you were in here."

Surly Jack saw his opportunity to criticize and said, "It looks to me like he hasn't gotten his hair cut since." The other patrons made token laughter sounds.

Brian eyed the man's shiny head and said, "And it looks to me like there's very little reason for you to even come here."

At that, the rude man turned red, acted like he was going to stand up and said, "Give me one good reason why I shouldn't take you out to the parking lot and punch you in the mouth."

Brian thought for a moment then said, "Well, I'd hate for you to give up your place in line and I don't want to mess up my hair."

The seated old men laughed noisily, which only increased Jack's anger. But, before things got out of hand, Craig stopped cutting hair and told Jack to calm down and Brian to find a seat. Then, before turning on the electric clippers added, "And besides Jack, you asked for only one reason; he gave you two." This time, everyone laughed and relaxed in his chair. Brian took a seat farthest away from the group and soon felt comfortable, warm and safe.

The next thing Brian knew, someone was shaking his shoulder. The barber said, "Wake up Brian, it's your turn. Everyone else is gone."

Brian jokingly asked, "Even the mean guy?"

"Oh don't mind him. Jack likes to think that he is a rough neck."

Brian sat down on the barber chair and said, "I've known a lot of guys just like him."

There were two barber chairs in the small building, but the only one ever used was the one nearest the restroom by the back door. A lighted revolving barber pole was mounted near the front door that was rarely utilized.

As Craig draped the apron around Brian's neck he said, "I suppose you want a butch."

Brian laughed and said, "Not quite that short. Block it in the back and leave it just long enough to make a part."

Faded photographs hung at eye level all around the paneled walls. Many were from successful fishing adventures, but most were memories of the grandchildren. Craig noticed Brian viewing the pictures and said, "Before I cut your hair, I should take your picture and hang it up there with the other local stars."

Brian thought about what his mug shot was going to look like in the near future and said, "I'm not sure that's a good idea, Craig. You might want to wait until the state cross-country meet this fall to get your celebrity picture."

Craig knew about Alex's condition and wondered if the high school runner would even be around come autumn time. As a barber, Craig heard all of the local gossip on every topic from many sources. But, he also had enough class not to question Alex's ability. Instead, he pointed at the wall and said, "I'll tell you what Brian, if Alex wins the state title, I'll hang his picture right over there. I've been saving that spot for something special."

Brian didn't respond so Craig changed the subject. "You know Brian, your hair is long enough you could donate it to one of those outfits that make wigs for young people being treated for cancer."

Brian nodded and said, "I like that idea. Hopefully, that's the only thing I donate this week."

After the haircut, while Craig swept the floor, Brian stood off to the side, looked in the mirror that encompassed the whole wall and evaluated his new look. Then he thanked the barber, paid the bill and added a tip. As he walked out the door, Brian felt invigorated. The nap had helped and as he drove home, he looked forward to finalizing his plans.

CHAPTER 3

During the drive home, Brian stayed on the backroads. He drove slower than normal because he didn't want to get into any trouble with the law on this day; that would happen soon enough. He had many regrets in life and wanted to savor this time and use it to reminisce about the good times and review the options left for him and his son. In his mind, he often asked his late wife for advice, but she never answered him. If not for his son and a few friends, he would have forgotten what love felt like.

FLASHBACK #1

The first time Brian ever saw Linda was at the end of the first day of their senior year at St. Steven's High School. He was walking down the hall towards the locker room and assumed she was heading for the door nearest the parking lot. As she walked ahead of him carrying an armload of books, Brian evaluated her movements. Because of the books, he couldn't tell if she had an economical arm swing, but her upper body was nearly upright with a slight forward lean. Her feet, which pointed straight forward, were lifted only high enough to clear the ground with each stride. There was little sway in her gait and other than the modest shimmy of her backside, he concluded that this girl moved very efficiently and could be a runner. He thought about pulling up along side her and striking up a conversation, but he wanted to see if she took the

142

bus home like an underclassman or if she got into a car. At least that is what he told himself. The truth was, he was shy and felt awkward around girls. Just when he summoned the nerve to catch up with her, a large figure appeared around the corner.

Mark Rashburn was a senior all state honorable mention lineman on the St. Steven's football team. At six feet one and two hundred and forty pounds, he was a big man on campus and if the teachers decided to fudge his grade point average, he would probably have another successful season and win a scholarship to a Division III college. Shaving ones head was not against the school's dress code, but wearing a sleeveless tee shirt was. Somehow he got away with it. Brian moved on past the oxen, but stopped short of entering the locker room in order to remain in earshot.

Linda had stopped so suddenly that she dropped half of her books. The large boy stood in front of her and blocked her way, but did not stoop to help her recover them. Instead, he grinned at her and said, "So, what time should I pick you up Saturday?"

She looked bewildered and said, "I don't know what you mean."

The oaf took on a condescending attitude and replied, "I can tell you're new at this school. There's a dance Saturday. I'm going to go to it. I figured you'd want to go with me. Make sense?"

Linda responded with a look of amazement and said, "You can dance?"

Mark blushed, then raised his voice, "That's not the point."

At that, Brian came rushing over and said to the football player, "Hey Rashburn, Coach Dripper wants to see you."

Mark gave Brian an irritated look and before he left, said to Linda, "We'll talk later."

Linda smiled at Brian and said, "Thanks, that guy is a royal pain."

"Oh, he's more than that. He's a bully and used to getting his way."

"I saw you standing over there, so I know that Coach What's His Name wasn't looking for his star player."

"It was all I could come up with in such a short notice."

Linda nodded and said, "By the way, I do like to dance. Tell me you know how."

Brian looked a little sheepish when he said, "I probably don't dance in the manner that you're accustomed to."

Linda pretended to be hurt and said, " What do you mean by that?"

"I mean I only slow dance. My grandma has been teaching me some dance steps."

Brian thought she was going to laugh at him, but she surprised him with, "That's so cool."

She then handed Brian her books, took out a pen and wrote something on a sheet of notebook paper. When she was done, she took back her books and handed him the folded paper. Before he could unfold it she gave him one last smile, headed for the door and said, "See you tomorrow, Brian Toth."

"How did you know my name?"

She winked at him and said, "You're more popular than you realize."

Brian watched her walk to a car and drive away. Only then did he look at the paper. On it she had written her phone number and the name, Linda Fejes. Brian stashed the paper in his pocket and floated to the locker room.

On Saturday at the dance, Linda and her sophomore sister Brenda, waited near a corner at the far end of the gymnasium away from the loud speakers of the DJ. Brian had gone into the hallway to retrieve cups of fruit punch and was held up by a chaperone who reminded him that drinks weren't allowed in the gym. Seeing this, Mark Rashburn strutted up to the girls and said, "Well, if it isn't the Duh sisters."

Looking disappointed, Linda said, "What are you talking about?"

"You know, Lin-duh, Bren-duh."

Brenda said, "That's really clever, Mark. Did you make that up all by yourself?"

Mark frowned and said, "I'm only trying to help you out here. Duh runner got stopped at the border by a guard, but I can get you chicks a drink. They won't stop me. All you have to do is say please."

Linda said, "Please excuse us." Then she grabbed her sister's hand and led her into the hallway.

A month later, late in the afternoon on Homecoming Day, Brian washed and cleaned the interior of his car. He then showered, put on some informal clothing and drove east out into the country until he found the address on Yondota road. There he turned into a long paved driveway that was lined on both sides with equally spaced red maple trees all the way to the house. Brian was worried about where he should park and settled for a spot off to one side away from the double garage doors. He sat there and noticed that the leaves were on the verge of changing into their autumn colors and he marveled at the home. It was a newer split level with pale yellow siding and light brown brick. Brian nervously checked himself in the rearview mirror and then left the safety of his car and walked to the front door. He felt anxious like he did at the starting-line of a race and dreaded meeting the parents, but what he really wanted most in life was on the other side of that door. He made a fist and knocked.

Brian was relieved when Linda opened the door. The dress code was casual, but she raised the standards. She wore a form fitting blouse and skirt with medium sized heels. Her chestnut colored hair was long and shiny and she smelled wonderful. As Brian gawked at her she said, "Are you coming in or are you just going to look at me all night?"

Brian stepped into the foyer and then said, "You look nice."

Linda closed the door and said, "Follow me."

She led him into the living room, sat him on a sofa and said, "I'll be right back. My mom wants to take a picture of us."

Brian sat still, but took the opportunity to scope out the room. All of the furniture looked brand new and there was a fireplace with a mantle that held many pictures. Just when he was going to stand up to get a closer look at the photos, Linda came back holding a camera. Her mother was right behind, holding a drink. At first Brian thought Linda had a twin, but as she got closer he could see slight wrinkles around her eyes and corners of her mouth. He stood up and said, "Hello, Mrs. Fejes."

She stepped close and shook hands. "Call me Janet," then added, "Would you like a drink? I made a large batch of this in the kitchen."

Brian blushed and said, "I better not, I'm driving you know."

Janet shrugged and said, "Well, I offered."

At that, Linda stepped forward and said, "Mom we have to get going, so how about taking our picture now?"

Janet said, "Why not."

Then Linda and Brian stood beside each other in front of the fireplace as several pictures were taken. Soon afterwards, Linda hurried her date out of the door and her mom shouted, "Have fun!"

They rode in silence for a while until Brian asked, "Where was your father?"

Linda hesitated, but then blurted out, "My father is a workaholic and my mother is an alcoholic, okay?"

Brian was a little shocked by this but waited for her to continue.

"There is no love in that house. Nothing Brenda or I do is ever good enough for my father. We have plenty of money, but my dad works as much as he can just to be away from us. My mother gave up a long time ago. I can't wait to leave, but I worry that Brenda will have to endure my share of the abuse."

All Brian could think to say was, "I'm sorry."

Linda stared at nothing and said, "It's not your fault. Funny thing is, that's the same thing I say to Brenda and myself."

Brian said, "I don't think it's so funny. Was it always like this?"

"No, I have some happy memories of our family when Brenda and I were very young. But, somewhere along the way, things changed. For some reason both of my parents became unhappy. They argued constantly over nothing. I think all of us hoped that moving to a new job, a new house and a new school would solve everyone's problems."

Brian thought, 'Wow, I thought I had issues,' but he said, "Before we go to the restaurant, I want you to meet someone who will cheer you up."

Brian drove her to a house in the Birmingham neighborhood of East Toledo where he lived with his grandmother. He brought Linda in through the back door and she noticed that the old house was small but tidy. As they walked through the kitchen and into the living room he held her hand. The old woman was sewing with a vintage Singer machine and didn't hear the young couple enter the room.

Brian turned to Linda and said, "This is my grandma."

"I figured that out."

The old woman still did not notice them, so Brian raised his voice, "Hello Grandma."

At that she stopped sewing, stood up and faced her grandson. When she saw Linda, her face lit up like a Christmas tree and she said to her, "Well, hello there."

Linda said, "Hi" and Helen Toth gave her the best hug she had in a long time.

Brian said, "Where's my hug, Grandma?"

The grandma released Linda and was swallowed by the embrace of her grandson. At six feet tall and one hundred and sixty pounds, Brian towered over his grandmother. She was only five-two and slightly overweight with mostly gray hair put up in a bun. He said to her, "This is Linda, the girl I've been telling you about."

Helen led them back into the kitchen where she sat them down at the table and served them Hungarian cookies and nut roll. She said to the teens, "Don't eat too much. You don't want to spoil your dinner. By the way Brian, where are you taking this attractive young lady?"

"I made reservations for supper at the Inn on the Bay and then the dance is in the gym."

"Oh to be young again!"

Linda smiled and said, "Mrs. Toth, what were you sewing in there?"

"I am making a sports coat for Brian. His last one is too small and please call me Grandma."

"Grandma, I wish I had your skills."

"Well, if you come back when you have more time, I'll teach you anything that you're interested in."

Brian sat quietly and was fascinated by how well the two women got along. Linda turned to him and said, "Brian, would you mind going to the dance by yourself tonight? I think I'd like to stay here with your grandmother."

"I think I would prefer to stay here with you two and skip the dance altogether."

The grandmother said, "You two are being silly and I think you better get going or you're going to miss all of the fun."

Brian and Linda said their goodbyes and were rewarded with hugs that only a grandmother can give. When Linda reached the car, Brian opened the door for her, but before she got in she turned around and returned the wave to the old woman who stood on the back porch. When they were on their way Linda said, "She's so nice."

Brian said, "I know, I've been living with her for ten years."

"Oh, what happened to your parents?"

Without showing any emotion, Brian told her, "They both died in an automobile accident when I was seven."

"So you're an orphan then."

"Don't say that. The other kids used to tease me about that in grade school."

"I'm sorry, Brian. That was thoughtless of me. There I was complaining about my lousy parents. I guess I should be grateful for what I have."

"Don't be sorry for me, Linda. I still have my grandma. And, I also have an uncle, though I don't claim him."

"Why not?"

"It's a long story."

"I have until midnight, Brian."

"Okay, Linda, let's just say that he's not been very nice to my grandmother. Times were tough when my father was raised, but my uncle was twelve years younger and the economy was much better then. So, Uncle Gene was a spoiled child and still acts that way. One time when I was about thirteen, he and my grandma were in the kitchen arguing about her will. He got so angry that he squeezed her forearms. When she cried out I ran into the room and pulled him away from her. He turned around, grabbed me by the neck and threw me down the basement stairs."

"Oh my God, Brian."

"It's okay now. I've grown since then and Uncle Gene is afraid of me now. He promised Grandma that if something happened to her, he'd let me live in the house for five years so that I can save for my own place. Time will tell."

Brian followed the shoreline of Lake Erie past the coal burning powerhouse where Linda's father worked and arrived at the crowded restaurant. They were seated near a window overlooking the waves pounding the sandy beach. There were many other students from the local high schools sitting around them. Brian and Linda recognized some of them but kept to themselves while they enjoyed each other's company and their meals. Afterwards, they went to St. Steven's for the dance. Upon entering the school they were greeted by class officers and chaperones. As they strolled down the corridor, everyone seemed pleasant and upbeat. Near the decorated entrance to the gymnasium, a group of football players loitered, expecting praise for their glorious Homecoming victory over archrival Clayton High the previous night. They ogled and loudly critiqued all who passed by. When it was Brian and Linda's turn to be taunted, Mark Rashburn said to them, "Linda, you're looking fine. Well, at least too good for him."

Brian wanted to respond, but Linda said to her date, "Ignore him, you're with me tonight."

They entered and gazed at the decorated gymnasium that was transformed into a wonderland with streamers and mood lighting. After mingling with the few girls who Linda had befriended and Brian's cross-country teammates, they found seats off to the side. From there they watched some guys, but mostly girls, dancing in the center of the room. During one song, Brian noticed that Linda was tapping her foot to the music and then asked her, "Did you want to go out there and dance with someone else?"

Linda tilted her head and said, "No, when it is time, I will dance with the one who brought me."

Fortunately, at this time the DJ decided to calm things down and played a collection of classic slow tunes, starting with Unchained Melody. Brian stood up and took Linda's hand and said, "It's now or never."

Linda was impressed with Brian's dancing abilities and was able to follow along easily. She was very pleased that Brian had taken the time to learn and basked in the looks they received from those nearby. The DJ alternated between sets of modern fast and vintage slow music. Brian and Linda danced to every slow song, but when the fast music was played they would relax, drink refreshments and talk to several students who praised them for their dancing talents. At one point when they were alone, Brian looked around the room trying to savor the event. When he looked back at Linda he noticed she was staring at him. Before he could ask her what she was thinking about she said, "Brian, I think you should take me home now."

They rushed to the car and when he pulled out of the parking lot asked, "Is everything alright?"

She didn't look at him but nodded as if a problem was resolved. Then she smiled and said, "Brian, I think I've learned more about you today than the whole previous month."

"Yeah, what else do you want to know?"

"I assume you have a job."

"I have two part time jobs, but between school and sports, I don't have much time to work after school. In the summer though, I work a lot of hours. That's how I could afford this car. I bought it from my grandma when she couldn't drive anymore. How about you?"

"Pretty much the same story as yours, only different. I babysit when I get a chance. Not so much for the money, mostly to see what a normal family looks like. I get to drive my mother's car because she lost her license."

Then they rode in silence until they reached her home. When he shut off the engine she asked, "What were you thinking about?"

Brian thought it might be a trick question but decided to be honest. "Besides you, one of the things I thought about was our upcoming meet on Tuesday at Pearson Park against Clayton. At last year's race I was worried about one guy and I wasn't sure if I was good enough to beat him. My grandma was still driving then and I was surprised that she came to watch the race. About five minutes before the start, I overheard that one guy make fun

of her. All the guys around him laughed and I knew
at that point that I would beat him or die trying."

"Tell me you won."

"I did. I ran hard and tried to hang on like I
always do, but he stayed with me and took the lead
when I made a wrong turn near the end.
Fortunately, I recovered, caught up with him and
sprinted by him. I did it for her."

"Good for you, Brian. Are you worried
about the rematch?"

"No. Ever since that day I'm no longer
worried about competition or even my uncle. I'm
not afraid anymore."

She gave him a look of admiration and then
got out of his car. He followed her to the front door
where she said to him, "Wait here a second. I want
to check on my mother, but it looks like no one is
here."

There were no lights on in the house, but
Linda made her way to the kitchen where she found
an unsigned note from her mother which read:
*Brenda is staying with a friend. Your father is
pulling an all-nighter so I caught a ride to the bar.
I should be home around three'.*

At that moment, Linda felt like crying and
wanted to be held. She tossed the note into the trash
and found Brian still waiting for her outside the
front door. He could tell she was upset and decided
he should probably leave. He awkwardly leaned

forward and gave her a quick peck on the cheek and then turned to leave, but stopped when she said, "I thought you weren't afraid anymore."

Brian quickly turned around, embraced her and planted a firm kiss on her lips. They stayed like that for a long time until Linda opened her eyes and said, "Wow, and you can dance too."

Brian laughed and said, "Right, but there are some things you shouldn't practice with your grandma."

Linda laughed at that and then again stared into his eyes. Finally, without a word she took Brian by the hand, brought him into the house and led him upstairs into her bedroom. After she lit a candle, they kissed again, this time more passionately. He watched her as she began to undress. Soon he followed her example and then they kissed some more and felt each other's bodies. He said to her, "Are you ready for this?"

"I am. And it's obvious to me that you're ready too."

She laid on her back across her bed and pulled him down on top of her. He did not have any protection to wear and wasn't sure how to broach the subject, so he just said, "Is it safe?"

She wasn't fully knowledgeable about contraception, but she was pretty sure 'it was safe'. Brian got his answer when she guided him inside her. He started off slowly, but when she began to rock her hips he increased the pace. In a short time the pleasurable experience was over. Brian wasn't sure what the protocol was after the big event so he just did what felt natural. He snuggled with and told Linda that he loved her and then he fell asleep.

Linda used this time to shower and put on her pajamas, robe and fluffy slippers. When she went back into the bedroom, she shook Brian awake and told him, "Wake up sleepy head. It's time for you to go home."

Brian shot out of bed and began dressing quickly. Linda said, "Relax Brian, we're still all alone."

After he was fully dressed, they scoured the room for any evidence left by the boy. Then they walked down the steps and out the front door to the spot where they stood a half an hour earlier. Linda said, "Now where were we?"

They shared a short kiss and when Brian went back for more, Linda stopped him and said, "Brian, I had a wonderful time tonight, but do the math. It's twelve-thirty."

"What do you mean?"

"We left a little early from the dance that was supposed to end at midnight. It's a good twenty minutes back to here. So you have to leave now or your grandmother will think ill of me."

"Oh, I didn't think of that."

"Another thing. If you mention what we did upstairs to anyone you will look like a real stud. I however, will be called the other four letter S-word. Please don't do that."

"Linda, what we did was beautiful. This was the best day of my life, but there is no way anyone will ever find out what we did."

The following Monday, Brian sat in the front row of Mr. Fehr's Drafting class working on the next assignment. The students referred to the teacher as 'Mr. Fair' because he was. He was also the dean of the boys and would miss the first half of this class to deal with an incident involving some football players at the Homecoming Dance. Unlike Brian, some of the students took advantage of this time to goof off. One of the slackers was Mark Rashburn who sat in the back row holding court on the events of the past weekend. It irritated him that Brian was getting ahead on the homework so he said to his pals, "Watch this."

His cronies took on a look of glee and excitedly anticipated what the large boy would do. Mark projected his voice to the front of the room, "Hey, Brian."

He paused and when he got no reaction he again said, "Hey, Brian."

Brian answered but did not look back, "What, Mark."

"Hey Brian. Saturday night, did you get any?"

This time Brian spun around in his seat and said, "Watch your mouth Mark."

"That's the difference between you and me Brian, I would have hit it."

"Watch your big mouth Mark."

The back row boys jeered and Mark began to walk towards Brian but turned around and sat back down when Mr. Fehr showed up.

After school the next day, the St. Steven's cross-country team ran to Pearson Park as a warm-up for their pending race against Clayton High. Linda had surprised Brian by not only being there to see the event, but also by bringing along his biggest fan. Linda had found a point on the course that offered a good view of the start/finish line and Helen Toth stood proudly beside her. The two teams were evenly matched but St. Steven's won by a point. Brian breezed to victory and set a course record.

Brian and Linda continued seeing each other at every opportunity. They spent Thanksgiving at Grandma Toth's house. Christmas was pretty much the same story. Linda's father worked, her mother drank and Brenda went to a friend's house. Brian had still not met Linda's father and was concerned about her mother and sister. Linda didn't want to talk about it and was in a bad mood when Brian picked her up at her house. Her attitude improved vastly though when they arrived at Brian's home. Grandma had prepared a feast for the three of them consisting of Chicken Paprikas, mashed potatoes and corn followed by an amber colored dessert wine which her late husband had created. Linda thought the wine was the best she had ever tasted, but she only took small sips. When dinner was over, all three helped with the dishes and the other kitchen cleanup chores. Then the time came for gift exchanges. Before dinner, Brian had given his grandmother a bouquet of flowers and now gave her a box of chocolates. Grandma gave Brian the finished sports coat which he put on and wore the rest of the night. She then gave Linda a gem-covered bracelet, which had been handed down, from her ancestors. Linda gifted the old woman a warm coat and matching hat and gloves and gave Brian a shirt and pants combination that went well with the sports coat. Lastly, Brian presented Linda with a thin gold necklace that held a small opal cross. As he clasped it around her neck, he told her that it belonged to his mother. She told him she would never take it off. Afterwards, they sat back down at the table and played numerous card and board games. Grandma brought out the wine again, but only she and Brian participated. Linda declined, opting for water instead. On the drive home, Linda was oddly quiet. Brian asked her if she didn't like the wine.

"The wine was very good and the food was excellent."

"Something's wrong, Linda. What is it?"

She looked at Brian then quickly looked away and said, "I missed my period again."

"What do you mean, again?"

"I missed it last month too."

As the weeks past by, the mild symptoms of morning sickness abated and with Brian's continuous reassurance that everything would turn out well, they were able to keep their secret. So far, Linda was able to avoid her parents, but as Valentine's Day approached, the rumors began to flow around the school. By March there was no denying the facts. All of the girls avoided Linda, but when she walked by, they would stare and share whispers. Most of the boys treated Brian in the same manner, but a couple had made disparaging remarks about his girlfriend. Both times, Brian defended her with his fists and received detentions for his actions. Eventually, the day came when Linda was called down to the office.

As a sideline, Margaret Shultz taught math classes at the school, but she preferred performing her duties as the dean of girls. Her goals were to advance her career and those of the few girls whose families donated to the endowment funds. She sat Linda in a chair across from her desk and then began the interrogation. "There's a nasty rumor going around that you and Mark Rashburn are an item."

"That's a lie."

"Then who's the father?"

Linda softly said, "Brian Toth."

Dean Shultz slowly shook her head and said, "Darn it, I was hoping it was a boy from another school."

When Linda didn't respond, Margaret said, "Well Linda Fejes, you leave me no choice. You're expelled. Gather up your belongings and leave."

Quietly, Linda got up and did just that.

Brian was unaware of the occurrence until later that day when Mrs. Shultz asked him to stay after calculus class. When all of the other students had left the room, she closed the door and confronted him. "About an hour ago I met with Linda Fejes and she said you were the father. Is that true Brian?"

"Yes it is."

"Then let me give you some advice. Her time here at St. Steven's is over, but you need to use your head and let her go."

"That's not going to happen."

"Brian, think about it. You have good grades. You're first team all-state in cross-country and you have a real good chance at winning state in the two-mile in track before you graduate."

"Mrs. Shultz, I'm begging you, please let her stay."

"You know what Brian, not everyone deserves a second chance. So, give your heart away, but use your head."

Before leaving the room, Brian sarcastically said, "Thanks for all of your help Margaret."

By then the next classes had begun and Brian walked down the empty hall to his locker. He left the school's books but gathered up the few things that were his. Before he made it to the door leading to the parking lot, Brian ran into Mr. Fehr. Along with the Dean was Mark Rashburn who had just been caught smoking in the locker room. Mr. Fehr said, "Where are you going Brian?"

"I have something to do."

Mark smirked and said, "Hey Brian, I heard the baby isn't yours."

Brian punched Mark in the nose and he dropped to his knees. Mr. Fehr stepped in between the two boys and said, "Brian, that's strike three. You're suspended for three days."

Before Brian walked to his car he said, "You're too late. I already quit."

Normally a law-abiding citizen, Brian exceeded the speed limit on the way to Linda's house. He found her sitting on a bench in the front yard. Beside her sat two pieces of luggage. Brian noticed that she was crying and said, "Where are you going?"

Linda stood up and reached her arms out to him. "I have to leave."

Brian held her tight as she sobbed. When she finally got her emotions under control, she relayed the story. "Before I got home, Mrs. Shultz called my mother and told her everything. Then my mom called my dad at work and he told her what to do. She packed my clothes, took back all of my keys and told me that I did not live here anymore. Apparently, she got her license back, because she took the car and drove away. Before she left she said she was going to bring Brenda home from school today and that it would be best for everyone if I was gone when they got back."

"Where would you go?"

"I've been doing some research. There is a school for unwed mothers up in Detroit. I don't have access to a phone right now, so I was going to ask one of the neighbors to use theirs. I can get a ride up there, but since you're here, you can take me."

"I'll give you a ride, but we're not going up there."

"Then where are you going to take me?"

"You're coming home with me Linda."

"I can't. Your grandma won't accept me like this."

"Listen, Linda, I've done some of my own research, but my investigation was about my family history. Regarding my grandmother, I found birth certificates and marriage licenses and once I did the math, I learned that she was married at the age of fifteen and with child. She is not aware that I know any of this and I want to keep it that way, but I do know that she will welcome you with open arms. At that, Brian picked up both suitcases and put them in the trunk. After he helped Linda into the car he said, "Besides, Grandma has been really curious about why I haven't brought you over for a visit lately."

Grandma Toth was overjoyed to see Linda again. Neither woman said a word to the other. Instead, they simply embraced and shared a good cry. Brian carried the luggage upstairs to the spare bedroom.

On the following Monday, Linda and Brian entered Wade High School. Grandma had made the arrangements for their transcripts to be sent to the public school and their first day was uneventful. Linda noticed that more than a few girls were in the same condition that she was. When they got home that day, they finished their homework in a short time and then Linda helped Grandma prepare the supper meal. Brian drove to a nearby foundry to talk with the owner about a job. The owner seemed like a friendly guy and the interview went well, so after he was given a pair of safety glasses, he was sent to the foreman's office.

George Wilson was a miserable man who liked to torment his workers. He only kept his foreman job because he cut corners when it came to safety and pushed the men for higher production. When Brian confided his situation and desperate need for a job, George knew he had him over a barrel. He told Brian that although he was underage and didn't have a high school diploma or GED, he would take a chance on him if he agreed to work for less money and benefits. Brian started work there the next evening. He was given the most difficult, dirty and dangerous jobs, but he didn't complain. George delighted in the abuse and would often short Brian on his paychecks.

Brian and Linda found the new homework to be much easier than at the prior school and both received all A's. Linda's doctor check-ups were all positive and she and Brian and Grandma loved feeling the baby move. The day after they graduated, Grandma went with them to the courthouse where they were married. The foreman had reluctantly given Brian the night off and after the three celebrated at a downtown restaurant, Helen was dropped off at her house. Brian and Linda proceeded to the Maumee Bay Lodge. After a good night's sleep and breakfast, they returned home and discovered that Grandma had moved Linda's things into Brian's bedroom.

A month later, Brian had the day off due to the Fourth of July holiday. The sun was beginning to set and Grandma, Brian and his very pregnant wife were heading out the door to go and see the fireworks, but then Linda's water broke. Helen went back into the house to retrieve the overnight bag as Brian loaded Linda into the car. While Brian carefully drove to the hospital he noticed that both he and Linda were breathing deeply. When they arrived, Linda was quickly taken away to be examined and then the nurse told Brian that the baby would be born that night. In the delivery room, Brian held her hand until the contractions became so intense that she said, "Don't touch me."

In between her final contractions, Linda said, "If it's a girl I'm going to name her Helen."

Brian said, "What if it's a boy?"

"If it's a boy, then you can name him."

At 10:42 the baby came into the world. Brian stayed at the hospital a couple of hours and then went home to sleep knowing that both Linda and the baby were healthy. In the morning, his grandmother awakened Brian. She was dressed and ready to leave and told Brian to hurry up because his breakfast was getting cold. Her urgent tone concerned Brian and he said, "What's wrong Grandma?"

"Nothing's wrong 'Daddy', I just can't wait to hold the baby. Let's go."

At the maternity ward, Great Grandma Toth held Alexander until he cried to be fed by his mother.

The conditions of Brian's home life were the best he had ever experienced, but the environment at work was just the opposite. Besides the constant aggravation from George, the air quality was really poor. Brian resumed running again just to clean out his lungs, but found himself entering and often winning local road races. The exercise, not only made him feel healthy, but also helped to relieve the stress of working at the foundry. When the weather was pleasant, Brian and Linda would take their son in a stroller for walks around the neighborhood. Sometimes Grandma would watch Alexander so that the newlyweds could go out to eat or see a movie.

Alexander liked to be held and only cried when he needed to be fed or changed. By the following spring, he learned to walk and brought much joy to the family. However, the bliss began to decline the night Brian arrived home after work and found a rescue squad parked in front of the house. Its lights were flashing and a few nosey neighbors stood on the sidewalk nearby. Brian rushed into the house and saw Linda holding Alexander. The paramedics were loading the still conscious old woman onto a gurney. Brian held her hand and said, "Grandma?"

She met his tear filled eyes and said, "This past year has been the happiest of my life." Then she was rolled outside and placed in the ambulance.

The next few days were a nightmare for Brian. Uncle Gene showed up for the funeral but didn't help with the expenses. Linda had told Brian that on the night that Grandma died, Uncle Gene had come over to mooch a meal. Linda couldn't stand to be around him so she had taken Alexander for a walk. Later, while on the back porch taking little Alex out of the stroller, she heard the uncle yelling at Grandma and telling her he needed more money. When Linda went into the house, the argument ended, but Grandma left the room for a short time and then came back and gave Uncle Gene an envelope. After he left, Grandma had a hard time catching her breath and had to sit down. She took some medicine and drank a glass of water, which calmed her down, but right about the time that Brian had gotten off work, she collapsed on the floor. To make things worse, two days later, Brian was fired from his job for an unexcused absence. After the burial, Uncle Gene approached Brian and asked Linda if he could have a moment alone with his nephew. Linda took Alexander by the hand and led him away a short distance.

"Brian, this all happened so suddenly, but that's the way life is sometimes."

It took everything Brian had in him not to hit the man. "This is all of your fault, Uncle Gene."

"We all have problems, Brian. But, what I want to talk to you about is this: The party is over. You have one more month in the house, but then you have to get out. I already have a renter lined up."

Brian glared at him and Uncle Gene decided not to push his luck any farther and he walked away while he still could.

On the way home, Brian and Linda had a long discussion and decided that the bad things that drove them away outweighed the good things that held them to the area. They agreed that they needed a new start somewhere else and to systematically research one region at a time until they found one that fit their needs. The next morning they gave Wood County a tryout. After a small breakfast, they put Alex in his car seat and pointed the car south. They chose the scenic route and followed the Maumee River until they reached Perrysburg. Along the way, they marveled at the old mansions and each of them chose a favorite that they said they would someday own. At Route 25 they turned left and headed towards the county seat, but just on the outskirts of Bowling Green, they got a flat tire. Brian pulled off to the side of the road as far as possible, put on his flashers and took out the jack from the trunk. As he was breaking the lug nuts loose, another vehicle pulled over behind him. A very tall figure with a crew cut exited the car and walked towards them. The man was smiling and wearing one of those white collars that Brian recalled seeing a Catholic priest wear, back in the days when he had attended church. Fresh out of the seminary, he introduced himself as Father Matt from St. Louis parish in B.G. and offered to help. In no time, the flat tire was replaced with the spare and then Brian followed the priest to a service station where the tire was repaired and reinstalled. Afterwards, Father Matt invited them to a meal at a nearby family style dinner where he patiently listened to their troubles. After lunch, he left them at the table and went to pay the bill. When he came back, he handed Brian a local newspaper that he had purchased at the counter. Father Matt explained to them that they would find housing and job opportunities in the classified ads, but he suggested they steer clear of the city because the rent was much higher there due to the presence of the university. He then invited them to attend church on Sunday and wished them well. Before he left, they profusely thanked the priest and then searched the paper for a place to rent and a job. Soon they found one of each.

A mile before they reached the center of the small city, they turned and headed west on Poe road. About nine miles into farm country, the road jogged and then they arrived at a row of older wood sided houses all painted white. They were situated on the edge of a large ravine with a small creek down below. Only one house was located across the road from the others and it looked run down. They both silently hoped that it wasn't the house for rent. The ad said to meet the owner at the address given. They pulled in and parked on the driveway of the large white house with a green roof and shutters. Young Alex had had enough of the traveling and wanted to be held. Linda soothed the boy and carried him around the yard and admired all of the flowering plants. Brian knocked on the front door and was invited inside by Martha McKee the landlady. He noticed that she moved very well for someone her age. She located the keys for the house next door and went outside to meet the rest of the family. As they toured the house, Brian saw that Linda looked very pleased if not relieved. The amount of rent Martha asked for was more than reasonable. The old woman told them that if they liked the house, the rent could be applied towards the purchase of the place. She added, that she wanted to surround herself with good people and normally was a fair judge of character, but she had made a mistake when she sold the house across the road. Martha then left the young couple to make their decision in private. Linda said to her husband,

"Brian, it's like a miracle. This place is perfect. I want to stay here."

"I agree. Let's just hope that the miracle continues and I find a job."

"Well, then before we tell Mrs. McKee the good news, use the phone there and see if you can land one."

Brian reviewed the ads and called a metal fabrication shop in the nearby small town of Weston. He was rewarded by a secretary who told him to show up the following morning at seven, wear work clothes and bring his diploma and lunch box. After Brian hung up, Alex giggled as his parents noisily celebrated. They couldn't stop smiling as they walked next door to pay Martha the first month's rent. Martha encouraged Brian to borrow her pick-up truck and drive back to Toledo to retrieve the few things that were theirs. As the old woman showered Alex with affection, Linda sat in a chair and a feeling of serenity came over her that she hadn't enjoyed in a long while and she knew she was home.

Brian had gotten into a routine of working, running and spending quality time with his family. They were friendly with all of the other tenants, but enjoyed spending time the most with Martha. All of the renters referred to her as the 'Mayor' since her ancestors built the tiny hamlet of McKee's Corners many years earlier after John McKee settled there in 1833. None of the neighbors liked Ron Bertman who lived in the house across the road from everyone. Ron didn't care what they thought and would rev his noisy engine long after sunset and burn garbage whenever the wind blew towards the white houses. He owned numerous guns and would target practice often, shooting at cans, bottles and varmints. Once in a while, he would stand out in the yard with a shotgun and blast away at songbirds. If it moved, it died. Sometimes, the wounded animals would make it as far as the road or onto the neighbor's yards where they would die and rot. Brian made several attempts to get on the guy's good side, but could never find it.

Life inside the Toth house was pure joy. Alex was growing fast, Linda was happy and Brian was, making a name for himself at the local running scene and eating well because Martha had greatly improved his wife's cooking skills. He did not bring home his problems from work though. Early on, he realized the conditions at Janco Metal Fabrication, were very similar to those of his prior job at the foundry. Same circus, but different clowns. Brian was encouraged to enroll at Owens College night school and was told by Foreman Don Heiler that learning to weld would benefit him. Brian completed the course and found out that the added skill benefited the company, but the raise never came. The only bright spot was that he was able to work the first shift. He assumed that every job must be like that and tried to get along no matter how bad it got because it paid the bills.

CHAPTER   4

Before Brian pulled into his own driveway, he glanced over at Ron Bertman's dump and figured that the only neighbor who knew or cared that Ron was missing, was Ron himself. Brian waved to Martha who was working in her garden and then looked passed her house to see if Nathan was around, but then realized he was still at work. Brian went inside his home to the kitchen and viewed the contents of the refrigerator. Recently, he had altered his diet by increasing his intake of fruits and vegetables. He wanted his body to be at the apex of health in the unlikely event that he would have to resort to Plan B. If it came to that, Brian seriously doubted that he possessed the courage to follow through with that tactic. He understood that anger could only push him so far. A run would make him feel better, but the effects of the nap had worn off and he needed more sleep. There was a small bottle of sleeping pills in the bathroom cabinet, but he rarely used them and wanted his body to be free from any drugs in his system. After he ate a large salad consisting of leafy greens, beets, tomatoes and nuts, he brushed his teeth, used the toilet and then after pulling down the shades, climbed into his bed. Brian knew if he lay there and tried to problem solve, he would never fall asleep. So he decided to think of something to distract his mind, something pleasant. He thought of his friend Nathan Kovacs.

Brian had returned to night classes at Owens College to study Electricity and Electronics. There he met Nate, who was unemployed and a recent high school graduate, and reminded Brian of

175

himself at that age. What Nathan lacked in experience, he made up for in effort. Against Brian's advice, he applied for a job at Janco and was hired on the spot. Brian wanted more out of life for Nathan but decided as long as he was working at the shop, he would teach him as much as he could and try to protect him. Brian took him under his wing because, over the years, he had seen many young people come and go. They had become disgruntled and left to search for something better. Brian often thought about leaving too, but the brainwashing tactics of the management always prevailed. He was led to believe that he had job security and was reminded that he would have to start at the bottom at the next job and if he left, would be given a poor reference. One day, after Nathan complained about how far he had to drive to and from work, Brian introduced him to Martha McKee.

When Brian awoke refreshed, he looked at the time and concluded if he killed two birds with one stone, he would be able to get in a run and still tend to his chores before the sun went down. He put on his running shorts, tee shirt, socks and shoes and began running west on Poe Road. When he reached Beaver Creek, he took a left and comfortably lengthened his stride to the Potterville location. When he arrived, he stood quietly at the corral and observed the ten mammals. Although all were covered with old horse blankets, they huddled together and seemed to avoid stepping on the clumps of dried manure. All of them were rather sedate except for the chubby specimen, which bellowed constantly. Brian chose to feed and water that one last because, not only was he obnoxious, but by the looks of him, the portly beast could afford to miss a couple of meals. When he was finished with the task, Brian spoke to them calmly to lessen their anxiety and then began the run back home as he considered their fate. Martha was no longer in her garden when Brian returned and although Nathan's car was visible, he was not. Lately, Nate had seemed overly concerned with his friend's mental state and Brian thought it would be best to avoid him. Brian showered and changed into the outfit that Linda had given him for their first Christmas together. He put on the sports coat that his grandmother had made for him and then drove to the hospital.

The visit to the hospital provided little comfort for Brian. Alexander's attitude was much better than his appearance and his energy level was at an all time low. Brian barely had any time to speak with him before his son fell asleep again. He had not received the assurance that he sought and dreaded the thought that it was possible, he would never see Alex alive again. The drive back home was a blur and he didn't recall entering the house, but he found himself sitting on his bed holding his Golden Rod tablet in his hands.

Brian scanned the list and then stood up and grabbed a pen and a red marker from the nightstand. He sat back down on the bed and drew a line under number thirteen with the marker and then wrote a message above and below it with the pen. His eyes floated up the list and stopped at numbers two and three. He felt so frustrated with these two guys because, although he was angry with and wanted to punish them, he couldn't because they were needed.

As he thought of the pair, Brian found he was unconsciously scratching out their names. When he realized what he was doing he stopped and thought about the man who was rated number one.

FLASHBACK #2

After Brenda graduated from high school, she visited and applied for scholarships at several colleges. The one she finally settled on was Bowling Green State University because they gave her the most financial aid. She had not chosen a field of study. Her prime objective was to get away from her parents, but living near her sister Linda was a close second. In order to expedite her departure, she signed up for summer classes and moved into a dormitory. Brenda enjoyed the freedom of college life, but just when her self-esteem began to improve, she met her future husband.

Ted Auffendor was the only son of a prosperous farmer who owned several hundred acres of fertile ground near the town of Haskins. He could have driven his new pick-up truck to the fair, but knew that his red convertible Mustang was a proven babe magnet. Due to unfortunate timing, Brenda's bus arrived at the ticket booth entrance just before Ted, who cut in line directly behind her. After he took a moment to look her over good, Ted took ten bucks out of his wallet and just as she was about to buy a ticket, he reached over her shoulder and slapped the bill on the counter. Brenda was startled, but Ted who didn't seem to care said, "Two tickets. I got this."

From there, Ted pulled her by the hand up and down the crowded walkways, skipping the rides, but visiting most of the livestock display buildings. Linda was never at a county fair before and found it all fascinating. Ted sensed that Brenda was a naïve girl and he wanted to exploit the fact. He knew a lot of people in attendance and to some of them, he introduced Brenda as his girlfriend. She was semi-flattered but noticed a higher percentage of the crowd made an obvious effort to avoid him. One time on the midway, they stopped to play a carnival game. Brenda stood back as Ted tried to impress her with his athletic abilities and then after failing to knock down all of the targets, bullied the kid into giving Brenda a large stuffed animal. She was embarrassed and wanted to refuse the prize, but Ted shoved it into her arms and said, "C'mon let's go for a ride."

Brenda followed him out of the fairgrounds, walked to the parking lot and stood on the passenger side of the Mustang. Ted got in on the driver's side and shouted at her, "Get in. Let's go."

They drove around the residential area on the new golf course and ended up at her dorm room where the first of many date rapes occurred.

Linda had many long discussions with her younger sister, but was unable to persuade her to date other boys. Ted had convinced Brenda that no one would want her after he had her and he threatened her with physical harm if she tried to leave him. Right after the fall semester, Brenda quit college and married the dirt bag. Ted downplayed education and made her his housewife in an old farmhouse, in the middle of nowhere, that his father owned. Brenda had agreed to give him as many offspring as he desired, but none ever materialized. Ted held her totally responsible for this lack of production and for retribution, he openly admitted to having fun with other girls. Brenda was grateful for the time alone during the nights of his adulterous behavior. Ted would almost never allow Brenda to go anywhere by herself. During the rare times she left the house, he was usually close by to monitor her actions. Linda noticed that Brenda rarely had an opinion, but often had bruises somewhere on her body. Ted spoke for his wife when necessary and she followed him around like a dog. Brian had wanted his wife to keep her distance from the uncouth puke, but Linda knew the only way she would ever get to spend time with her sister was to put up with the abuse.

Brian was aware there were a lot of cruel people in the world, but he knew the one who could hurt him the most might be himself. With mild satisfaction, he drew a line through Ted's name and placed the list on the nightstand and then set his alarm clock. Brian didn't want to miss what might possibly be the most important day of his and his son's life. As he lay in his bed, Brian reviewed his life. He cherished the good times with Linda and Alexander and as he relaxed, his mind drifted off and he entered the dreamland. He dreamed he was floating up towards the sky and witnessed the clouds open to allow light to shine down and show him the way. As he rose higher, any anxiety he felt melted away and he saw a figure in the clearing. The closer he got, the more the details came into focus. She had chestnut colored hair, wore a blue dress and hovered with her arms reaching out to him.

AFTERWORD

On the wall at Craig's barbershop in Portage
Ohio, hang two framed pictures. One is a black and
white photo of a longhaired man in his mid thirties.
The twinkle in his eyes and the smirk on his face
suggest that he knows a secret. Adjacent to that
frame is a colored picture of the man's son taken the
moment he crossed the finish line of the state cross-
country meet. The high school boy has his arms
raised above his head as a sign of triumph. There
are other figures in the print, but because they are so
far back, they are small and blurry. Under his shirt,
the runner has a large scar that he carries like a
badge of honor.

REDEMPTION DAY

CHAPTER 1

Looking down into the room, Brian watched as several members of the SWAT team burst through the game room door. He sensed their disappointment as they pointed their guns at the dying man on the floor. After the two surgeons were released from their bondage in the chairs, Brian experienced a floating sensation. He could not see well because now he was enveloped in thick dark smoke. Soon his feet touched solid ground and he began to walk. He was unsure of the direction, but suspected he was close to something very dangerous and wanted to keep moving. The hope he had, that this was just a dream, quickly evaporated when he distinctly heard evil voices behind him. When he looked back, the smoke cleared just long enough to allow a glimpse of several hideous looking man-like creatures and he realized it was more than a nightmare. They were carrying sickles and torches and dragging lengths of rusty chains. As they closed in on Brian, the demons reached out for him with dirty, long clawed fingers. They made pitiful celebration noises and screamed at him to stop. Contrary to their demands, Brian began to run like there was no tomorrow. His strong effort allowed him to pull away from the attackers, at least for the moment. For the first time in a long time, he worried about his own well-being. The smoke turned into fog and the frightening sounds diminished until he only heard his own

footfalls and breathing. Brian started to feel
fatigued, but he didn't dare let up.

Seventy-six year old Alexander Toth was
resting in a bed on the second floor, in a calmly lit
room, next to a park in Bowling Green. Soothing
sounds of waterfalls and songbirds were cascading
from the ceiling speaker. The prevalent atmosphere
of the room suggested it was a place for a relaxing
massage. It was not. It was a hospice, a place
where people came to die, as comfortably as
possible. The tired looking man was hooked-up to
an I.V. There was an oxygen tube under his nose
and electrodes were attached to his chest, exposing
a large scar. Numerous pieces of equipment next to
the bed, that were blinking and beeping, monitored
his condition. The screen showed the pulse of his
elderly heart.

Normally there was a limit to the number of
people who were allowed to visit a patient, but that
policy was broken everyday during the past week.
Friends from near and far came to drop in on
Alexander one last time. Today though, only family
members were allowed in the crowded room.   All
six of his children stood around the edge of the bed.
Behind them were most of their spouses,
Alexander's grand children and their kids, many of
which spilled out into the hallway. They all deeply
loved the man and although he wanted this to be a
joyous occasion, a few of them wept openly.

CHAPTER   2

Suddenly, Brian was aware of his surroundings. He was standing on a flat, dirt country road taking a short break. There were no utility poles or any hint of civilization. The temperature and humidity seemed to be on the high side. He felt grateful to have on only a tee shirt, running shorts, socks and shoes. In the distance he saw a woodlot on both sides of the road and noticed another runner heading his way fast. For a second, Brian considered turning around and high tailing it back where he came from, but the thought of the pursuing beasts convinced him to take his chances with the lone being. When they were in earshot of each other, the stranger told Brian, "Keep running."

Brian obeyed the order and the man turned and dropped in along side of him, matching his strides. Nothing else was spoken as they plodded down the road. Brian stole glances at the athlete and felt that some how he knew him, but could not figure out who he was. The foreigner anticipated his questions and said, "Yes you know me, Brian, and I'll come right to the point. You've really ticked me off lately." Brian eased up a little on his pace and said, "Who are you?"

"Don't let up. They're still coming for you. Oh, and how do I know these things? I was assigned to you back when you were an innocent boy. God knows I tried to keep you safe, but noooo, you had to go off the deep end. You made me look bad, Brian. There were those who said I should just let you fall on your face. Why do I keep trying to save you? I don't know. Maybe I'm just as big of a moron as you. Or, maybe I take pride in my job and want to boost my winning percentage. It could be that I like the challenge and hope for a promotion. Then again, I probably just care too much…"

Brian never stopped looking at him and realized the stranger was talking mostly to himself. For a second time Brian said, "Who are you?"

The runner starred at him and said, "I think you already know."

Recognition finally dawned on Brian. "You're my guardian angel."

All conversations, which were already reduced to hushed tones, stopped completely when the monitor's alarm went off. Alexander's heart had missed a couple of beats and his children anxiously looked between their father and the screen. Alexander broke the silence, "Not yet."

While some of the family chuckled, others just frowned. Alexander pushed on. "Come on, lighten up. I'll tell you what. When I pass, the first one of you that imitates Porky Pig and says, 'That's all folks,' can have my car.

Nobody responded and the silence was broken when a nurse came in and silenced the alarm. She said, "Mr. Toth, Alexander, there's someone in the hallway who wants to talk with you."

Alexander's oldest son, who went by the nickname, 'Sonny' said, "Well, who is it?"

The nurse looked at Alexander and said, "He's a ninety-six year old man in a wheelchair, but he won't give me his name."

Alexander said, "Send him in."

The family's curiosity grew and as they made room, the nurse guided the wheelchair through them and parked it at the near side of the bed. For a while, Alexander studied the old man and then smiled and reached out and shook his hand.

"Kids, this is the man who saved my life, Dr. Erikson."

CHAPTER 3

The fog slowly uncovered the topography. Brian felt the effort became slightly easier and saw that he had begun a long decline into a beautiful valley. When he turned to speak with the angel, he was gone. Brian savored the slope and took in the view. The scenic landscape was sprinkled with colorful flowering bushes and the lush green grasses were contrasted by the brown dirt road. Here and there were large granite boulders. Brian could not tell if he had been running for hours or days. Eventually, the road leveled out and the angel again accompanied him. They ran together for some time before the angel spoke. "I forgot to tell you the rules."

Brian kept his mouth shut and listened as the angel continued. "You have to keep running, no matter what. I think you know what will happen to you if you stop. You cannot help anyone else. Any other soul that you see is doing penance. Their sentence may or may not be eternal. Either way, it's none of your business. You only need to concern yourself with saving your own soul. By the way, I can read your mind so I know you have a lot of questions, but you'll have to ask them if you want me to answer. Also, there may be some inquiries that I'm not allowed to respond to. Okay, go ahead, ask away."

"What is your name?"

"You can call me Samuel, but not Sam."

"Samuel, I'm sorry for all of the grief I've cause you."

"Tell it to the Judge, Brian."

"I hope to have the opportunity."

"Well, don't get your hopes up too high. Your case isn't looking very good."

"Could you expound on that?"

"Let's start with your dealings with Father Matt. You have the right to question the Church and its priests, but you went way overboard. So I'm going to leave you to your thoughts for a while to ponder that subject."

Brian looked at Samuel and noticed that no matter the effort, the angel never sweated or even breathed hard. "Samuel, before you go, I need to know. After all I've sinned, why haven't you given up on me?"

The angel solemnly appraised Brian then said, "Because, I was not able to take care of my mother in her old age, but you did and so did your family."

"Your mother was…"

Before Samuel dematerialized, he finished Brian's thought. "Yes, my mother was Martha McKee."

Sonny verbalized what all the children were thinking. "Dr. Erikson, this room would be empty if not for you."

While the family listened intently, Alexander and the retired surgeon exchanged pleasantries. They swapped stories until Dr. Erikson's face took on a serious expression. "Brian, for a man your age, your body is still in tremendous shape. You might be a candidate for another transplant. Have you considered that?"

Sonny jumped in with, "We've tried to convince him."

Alexander cut him off with a look. "Yes, I have thought of that, doctor. Are you and your partner still trying to drum up some business?"

"Not at all. I retired a long time ago and apparently you didn't know about Dr. Bauhner. Ironically, he died shortly after your operation. If the timing was a little bit different, you could have ended up with his heart."

"I wouldn't have wanted his heart."

"As it turned out, some crooked politician got it, but was then sentenced to prison for sixty years. What a waste."

"On all accounts."

"Anyhow, I never told anyone this, but Dr. Bauhner didn't want to sign up for the donor program. I had to shame him into it. Then, the funny thing is, he went and got himself killed by a jealous husband. The not so funny part is that the husband beat me to it."

CHAPTER 4

Brian ran on alone. The brown dirt road took on a darker, almost black tone. He assumed that was because the valley contained more organic matter, judging from the soil color and the healthy plants around him. It was just an observation-knowledge he had gained in the prior world, something that had no value for him now. After putting off the assignment as long as he dared, Brian focused on his memories of Father Matt.

FLASHBACK #1

The priest was a likable man who would always begin his homilies with a clean joke. Brian chuckled aloud thinking of those times. He put aside his positive reminiscences and reviewed the bad ones. After shifting through the most shameful recollections, he concentrated on a particular day in Cleveland. Father Matt had organized a bus trip to the art museum there to view paintings concerning the Afterlife, but only a dozen people showed up for the fieldtrip. Of the twelve, one was a loud-mouthed egotist who dominated the conversations. Brian left him with the group near the front of the bus and took a nap in the back. During the ride there, the rude man convinced most of the group that they should first visit the Cathedral while in the city. Father Matt reluctantly put it to a vote and hence, the visitation of the museum was reduced by two hours. The realization that he wouldn't be able to fully take in all of the artwork put Brian in a sour mood.

Everyone was hungry when they finally arrived at the museum. Father Matt directed them to the cafeteria and was going to join them until Brian indicated that he was going to use the remaining time to view paintings. The large priest 'offered-up' the hunger pangs and joined him. At the Cathedral, Brian wanted to ask Father Matt numerous questions about the Church and its teachings, but never had the opportunity until now. As they strolled from room to room, Brian began to grill the priest with pointed questions. "Father Matt, what if everyone is right?"

"About what, Brian?"

"Is it possible that after death, the Christians will either go to Heaven or Hell, the other religions will go to whatever they believe and the atheists won't go anywhere? For them the lights will go out and there will be nothingness. Your reality will be what you believe it will be. How does anyone know for sure what happens after death?"

"It all comes down to faith. The Biblical scholars have taught us that there will either be a reward or a punishment."

"Can good deeds erase bad ones?"

"Good deeds will go a long way, but you need to confess your sins to be forgiven."

"Can saints really intercede?"

"Yes, much evidence of this nature has been well documented."

"Are there different levels of Heaven?"

"In all of my studies of our religion regarding the afterlife, I have never come across any information on the subject."

"Is Notre Dame really God's team?"

Father Matt laughed. "I'm glad you still have a sense of humor."

"I was just checking to see if you were paying attention."

"Next question."

"How do we know if God hears us?"

"Well, you know when your prayers are answered, and if not, keep praying."

At that point the two men arrived at a disturbing painting entitled Judgment Day. Some of the people on the framed canvas piece were being guided up into Heaven by angels. The others were being roughly thrown into Hell.

"Father, once you die, are there any second chances?"

"I wouldn't bet on it, Brian."

Before Brian could question the priest any further, the group from the cafeteria caught up with them. Father Matt said, "Brian, you seem to have a lot of doubts about your faith. Give me a call next week sometime so I can help you resolve your issues."

CHAPTER 5

Brian held a strong pace as the road paralleled a small stream. He thought of the many counseling sessions and felt guilty about not always trusting the advice the priest had often given him. Samuel appeared and joined him as the stream widened. "Brian, have you begun to feel it?"

"Do you mean the fatigue or the guilt?"

"Well, both."

"Samuel, I have a lot of remorse for all of the mistakes I've made in life. And yes, I'm getting a little tired too."

"Good, keep going. By the way, you're going to pass by a man up ahead who has been ordered to complete a task. He has been commanded to dig nine graves, six feet deep."

"What did he do to deserve that punishment, if I can ask?"

"During his life he was a mass murderer. He killed nine people."

What Brian thought, the angel anticipated. "Yes, that could have been you had you gone that route."

Brian said, "Thank God for small miracles."

"Watch yourself there, Brian."

"Sorry, go ahead."

Samuel pretended like he was going to slap him. "You're on thin ice here Brian. Take my advice- do not stop to help that man dig. He is always optimistic that he can finish the job but it never happens. Whenever the man gets close to completing the task, he tires and falls asleep. When he awakes and goes back to work, he finds that the holes are all filled in and he has to start over."

"Will he ever succeed?"

"I think you know the answer. One more thing before I leave. Even here, remember that temptation is great and will hurt you. The man is very convincing and will try to acquire your help. So to help get past him, I want you to revisit another memory of yours. Sometimes good deeds can overshadow the bad ones. Think back about what happened at the festival in Tontogany. You did a really good thing that day, Brian. I was proud of you."

FLASHBACK #2

The Drone Eviction Festival in Tontogany was originated by a small group of women who preferred the company of other women. They celebrated, the yearly eviction of all male honeybees from the hives, by drinking Meade wine and swapping boastful tales of conquest. The drones, which were fed and cleaned-up after by the female worker bees, were the only male occupants of the hive. The sole purpose of the drones was to inseminate the queen bee. When the cold weather of late autumn began and their services were no longer required, they were unceremoniously thrown out. The life of leisure was over; hardships and certain death outside of the hive awaited them. Any attempts by the drones to re-enter were blocked by over-zealous female worker bees. 'Bee bread', commonly referred to as Hungarian nut roll, was made and sold by the local Woman's Club. However, as the gala evolved, the director was no longer a man-hater and men were allowed to attend and encouraged to don drone costumes while the women re-enacted the evictions. The money raised during the annual celebration was donated to local women's organizations. Later, when a 5K-charity race was added, Brian would usually enter and win.

One year, Brian was recovering from an injury and decided to use the race as a training run. The course consisted of two laps around the perimeter of the small town. There was a wide range of talent levels in attendance and Brian recognized some of the local high school and college runners warming up near the starting line. One of the runners that he noticed was a sixteen-year-old boy who had entered the race the two prior years. The kid, who had lined up in the back row, was small for his age and suffered from muscular dystrophy.

After the starting pistol was fired, some of the runners were able to hang with Brian up until the one-mile mark. However, he soon opened up a gap and was applauded by a gauntlet of spectators as he glided down Main Street. During the second lap, when Brian reached the two-mile mark, he felt fresh and injury free, so he pushed it to the end. As he approached the finish line, Brian saw the last place runner limping along, just beginning his second lap. Normally after he finished a race, Brian would jog back towards the incoming runners to cheer them on, but this time he had another plan. He waited at the finish and after congratulating his fellow racers, he asked a favor of them. The race director enthusiastically agreed to re-stage the finish area. By the time the second-from-last runner arrived, Brian had accumulated a large mob of volunteers and they all ran back out on the course to escort the final racer. The runners patiently encouraged the boy and when they arrived at Main Street, the cheering crowd was larger than when Brian had finished. With one hundred yards remaining, all of the runners dropped out and left the young man 'sprint' to the finish all alone After the runner broke the tape, Brian took his ribbon with the first place medal and draped it around kid's neck. The other finishers congratulated the boy and he was made the centerpiece of many photos. When Brian had tried to slip away unnoticed, the boy's parents met him. They thanked him heartily for all he had done, especially for donating his first place medal. Brian shrugged and said, "He worked the hardest of any of the runners today; he deserved it."

CHAPTER 6

It was only midmorning and the alarm went off for the third time when Alexander's heart fluttered. Dr. Erikson said, "I always hated that sound. This would be a good time for me to leave. I hope to see you again somewhere, Alex."

The nurse arrived to shut off the monitor noise and then pushed Dr. Erikson out of the room. Alexander's oldest daughter took the opportunity to relay a message to him. "Dad, Mom just texted me to tell you that she will be here around lunch time. After church, she met the new priest and then volunteered to help move another customer into the Haskins House. She wanted me to make sure I told you to, 'Hang in there'."

Alex laughed, but no one else did. "That's an inside joke, kids. I used to tell her that whenever she was having labor contractions. She finally got me back."

After her son left for the priesthood and in honor of her sister Linda, Brenda opened up her home for first-time pregnant women who needed a place to stay. Known as the Haskins House, the eighty-acre farm was a work-for-stay organization. The residents were housed, fed and tutored in exchange for tending to the large fruit and vegetable gardens, livestock and house chores. The work hours were from sun up to sun down and all abled bodies helped out wherever needed. Upon birth of the baby, the mother and child were moved to another compassionate location. All of the women

understood the deal and were grateful for the
accommodations, advice and loving care given by
Brenda Fejes. Law allowed only thirteen women at
one time in the home. The waiting line for
acceptance into the house was long.

About noon, Alexander's wife, Ann still had
not arrived at the hospice. Alexander's midday
meal arrived on a cart and as he slowly ate it, he
suggested to the visitors that they all go out for a
long lunch somewhere. They saw that he looked
weary and would take a long nap soon. After a
short conference, they agreed to return at a set time
and left Alexander to rest in peace.

Before Alexander fell asleep, his mind
drifted back to the days of his original heart.

FLASHBACK #3

The shock of his mother's recent death had
slowly eroded away, but he doubted the sudden
attacks of grief would ever let him be. He and his
father made a deliberate effort of resuming a normal
life, but all of the things left behind by Linda made
it difficult. Everyday when Alexander went to
school, Brian would search for work. Sometimes
they would run together and have in-depth
discussions about the future and the past, during
which time they both tried not to cry. Eventually,
Brian decided to give away much of Linda's
belongings. He wanted to retain things with
sentimental value like pictures and jewelry but

donate clothing and items that held no significance. After they had rounded up all of her articles, Brian selected a box full of some of the finer things. Besides clothing, he decided to put a few pictures and pieces of jewelry into the container and asked Alex to take it over to his aunt's house.

Alexander placed the treasures into the Cavalier and headed towards Haskins. He didn't know all of the details, but sensed reluctance by his father to make the trip. Alexander knew his dad had a civil relationship with Aunt Brenda, but not with her husband Ted. He had witnessed several episodes of uncivilized behavior by his uncle and hoped he wouldn't have to deal with him. Alexander felt relief when there was no answer at the front door, but just when he was going to set the package on the porch and leave, Uncle Ted opened the door. He had a can of beer in his hand. "What do you want?"

"I have some things for Aunt Brenda. Is she home?"

"I don't know where she's at. I do know she didn't make me breakfast before she left, so I'll have to talk about that with her when she gets home. What's in the box?"

"These are some of my Mom's nicer things. My Dad thought Aunt Brenda would appreciate them."

The drunken man chugged the rest of his beer and then tossed the can into the flowerbed. "Well, I have no idea why she would want someone else's junk, but she's not very bright. Just leave it on the porch. I don't want any of your bugs in my house."

Alexander placed it near the porch swing, avoided eye contact with his uncle and descended the steps. As he reached the car he turned around when Uncle Ted shouted at him. "Hey Alex, my two aunts had heart trouble. Your mom just didn't fight hard enough."

CHAPTER 7

The stream widened and the dark fertile soil was replaced with heavy clay. The terrain was void of all trees and even the weeds looked anemic. Up ahead, near the side of the road opposite the waterway, Brian saw a tall, lanky man digging a hole with a shovel. The scraggily man wore a hateful scowl on his face, but that expression changed to pleasant and likeable when he saw the lone runner approach.

Like a used car salesman, the sweaty and dirt covered man acted as if he was Brian's best friend. Each sorrowful plea caused Brian to slow down a little bit more. Like a siren, he used several tactics to try and get the runner to stop and help him dig. Brian nearly came to a complete stop when the man transformed himself to resemble the sixteen-year-old boy with muscular dystrophy. Fortunately, Brian was not fooled by the dirty ploy. Instead, he remembered the advice of the angel and ran past the evil man.

Upon leaving the cemetery area, Brian felt a little stronger and had a bounce in his step. The river widened and its current strengthened, the lush vegetation returned, as did the angel. Very colorful birds sang and flew nearby the two runners as they travelled over rolling hills and scenic curves. Large fluorescent butterflies flew with them as they covered mile after mile. While they were traipsing through a glen loaded with daffodils, Samuel finally broke the silence. "What did you think when you saw the grave digger?"

"You know what I thought. I was glad it wasn't me. It could have been me if things turned out differently."

"You lacked patience and weren't rational at times."

"Is that a sin?"

No, but those deficiencies led you to sin. Think about the top thirteen on your list that you brought harm to."

As Brian was contemplating the memory, he spied a water puddle just ahead. When they reached the obstacle, instead of avoiding it, he splashed through it intending to douse Samuel. Unfortunately, the angel repelled the water and Brian was drenched instead.

"Are you done playing games now, Brian?"

Brian was embarrassed and shocked by how cold the water was. "Yeah, sorry. What was the question again?"

They ran on and as Brian drip-dried the angel said, "I'd like for you to meditate about your actions and how they affected those thirteen victims."

In his mind, Brian systematically reviewed his relationships with each of the thirteen people. He still felt anger towards Ted, but not so much concerning the two doctors or the other ten. Well, maybe Don Heiler. He still held a grudge against him.

The road finally exited the valley and its river and recast itself into a series of long switchbacks up a massive tree-filled mountain. The incline caused Brian to shorten his stride and pump his arms slightly more, but there was no strain on the face of the angel when he said, "The logic that committing a crime would bolster your son's chance for a heart transplant was horribly flawed. Though your thinking was preposterous, your heart was in the right place. No pun intended."

Brian shook his head to show his disapproval as Samuel continued his lecture. "I like dogs, Brian. So, in my opinion, for killing your son's dog, I think Ron Bertman should have been higher up on the list. And another thing, I probably shouldn't be telling you this, but turning Ted into a gelding caused quite the commotion back where I reside. Despite themselves, all of the other angels had a good chuckle and even God just shrugged his shoulders."

"So Samuel, are you suggesting that there may be hope for me?"

The angel didn't answer the question directly. "Brian, how did you feel when you left the grave digger back there?"

I felt a little bit fresher for some reason."

"That was because you did the right thing. Whenever you obey God's will or show remorse, you will feel better. Remember, the pestilent ones

207

are still hunting for you. I am pulling for you, but the final step will come if and when you experience forgiveness. In time, as you perform penance, all of your bad thoughts will erode away. The memories of all incidents involving evil people will be erased. All that you will be left with will be a total sense of pure joy."

"What will happen to all of the bad people?"

"You don't want to know. And besides, it won't matter to you because all memories of them will be gone.

"So, there is hope for me."

"Yes, there is a chance that your soul will be cleansed."

"How long will it take?"

"I wouldn't tell you even if I did know. That's part of the deal. All I can tell you is that you have a chance if you do the penance. So, I suggest you stay positive and keep making an effort."

"Right. What other choice do I have?"

"You don't want the other option." Then the angel disappeared.

CHAPTER 8

When Ann arrived at the hospice, she found the room was void of all visitors. She stood at the side of the bed and used the quiet moment to gaze down at her sleeping husband. There were still a few things that she wished to say to him in private, but decided to wait until he was done napping. Until then, she would sit in a chair, be by his side and remember the good times.

FLASHBACK #4

After Alex had received his new heart and was well enough to resume normal activities, he was released by the hospital. Aunt Brenda had welcomed her nephew into her home, but he graciously declined the offer. Instead, Alex returned to McKee's Corners and moved in with Martha. When he was cleaning out his prior residence, an old paperback was found in his father's closet. In the summer, Alex read that book, *The Heart of a Champion* by Bob Richards and began training again. With medical approval, Alex rejoined the Otsego high school cross-country team and flourished. After the state meet, he received numerous full ride scholarships from a variety of universities. To his dismay, Alex sensed that most of the colleges were only interested in him because of the novelty of having a heart transplant recipient on their team. He did not want to be part of a freak show. He did want to stay near elderly Martha, Aunt Brenda and cousin Sam. Very few people knew that Alex and Sam were really half-brothers. While recuperating in the hospital, Alex came to the conclusion that he wanted to teach and coach runners at the high school level. When Alex had visited Ohio Northern University, he liked the small campus and the degrees that were offered. He met with the cross-country coach who bluntly informed Alex that he was not interested in his notoriety. He went on to say that Alex would not receive any special attention and would have to earn his spot on the team. Alex liked him immediately.

For her age, Martha was still mobile and clear thinking, and because the college in Ada was only one hour away, Alex came home as often as he could to help her. She would reward him with a home-cooked meal and listened to his success stories, both in the classroom and in athletics. Every visit always included an inquiry about obtaining a young lady with future wife potential. Alex had dated a few hopefuls, but always had to shake his head when asked that question by Martha. But then, just two weeks from graduation, he found himself in line at the local pizzeria. It was a very pleasant spring day and the joint was crowded with students. Alex was at the counter picking up a takeout order for him and his roommate. He turned to leave, but then stopped in his tracks. There in front of him was the most attractive girl he had ever seen. She had natural blond hair, was wearing shorts, sandals, and an ONU tee shirt and was holding a thick book. She smiled at him and for the first time in his life, Alex was tongue-tied, but she saved him with, "What are you having?"

He quickly recovered, "A large pepperoni with mushrooms. There's too much here for me. Would you like to have some?"

While she considered the offer, Alex looked around the room and saw that all of the tables were occupied. Before she could decline, he said, "It's too crowded in here and it's such a nice day. We should go across the street to the park with the caboose and enjoy it there."

She said, "I would like that."

Even though they started college the same year, Ann had to complete the remaining Pharmaceutical classes and internships, two years after Alex had graduated. During that time, they saw each other frequently. After a few interrogations, both Martha and Aunt Brenda approved of the relationship. There were a few incidents of disagreement during the courtship, but they were mild and easily resolved. Alex had landed a teaching and coaching job at his former high school. Ann had a position waiting for her at a Bowling Green pharmacy, pending achievement of the state board certification.

A few months before Ann graduated, Alex drove down for a visit. They took a walk on the 'green mile' trail while Ann updated Alex on her current internship and the latest news about her mom, dad and seven siblings. Alex was always envious when she talked about her large family. He stopped her in the middle of the small woodlot and said, "Ann, I wish I had a big family like you do."

She looked him straight in the eyes and said, "Then you should work on that."

"Marry me, Ann"

"Alexander Toth, I will marry and always be there for you."

CHAPTER 9

Brian continued up the mountain at a steady pace, but he began to feel fatigued in various muscle groups of his body. To counter the effect of his tiring effort, he rested some parts by altering his body lean, arm swing, foot placement, stride length and breathing. But, despite these changes, exhaustion and thirst were taking its toll on his body and he wondered how much longer he could hold on. He tried to distract his mind from the reality of the situation and thought he had achieved his goal when he visualized a pure white horse trotting beside him. The large animal was strong looking and came equipped with a comfortable-looking leather saddle. Hanging from the saddle horn was a canteen, which Brian presumed, contained water. Brian could tell it was cold and full because he was allowed to touch it, but every time he tried to remove it, the horse would move away. Near the point of collapse, Brian considered hopping up on the horse and swallowing the entire contents of the container, but then he looked at his hands and saw that the palms were coated with white paint. It finally dawned on him that things weren't as they appeared. The realization that he was again being tormented by temptation fueled his rage and he forcibly slapped the horse on its flank. The animal leaped into the air and transformed into a winged, scaly dragon. The beast released a demonic scream, and then before flying out of sight, it looked down on Brian with hateful red eyes and singed the runner's hair with its flaming breath.

Ann reached over and touched Alexander's hand and softly said, "I kept my promise; I'm still here for you."

Alex awoke, briefly scanned the room and said to his wife, "Did you say an extra prayer for me at church this morning?"

"What did you think I was doing there? Besides I'm pretty sure you already have a fairly clean soul."

"You don't know everything about me."

"Well, if you have something to confess, the new priest will be here shortly."

"I liked the last priest we had. It's too bad his life had to end like that."

The recent demise of old Father Matt was the result of an over-exuberant celebration following a close win on a local tennis court. After holding off a torrid comeback by an elderly nun, who suffered from rheumatism and partial blindness, the tall priest attempted to jump over the net. He would have cleared the barrier had he not tripped over his own feet and landed on his head.

"Yes that was a sad day, but I think you're going to like his replacement. And, he can hear your confession right here if you feel the need."

Alex put on his serious look and said, "I'm not going to bother him with it, but I am willing to tell you what happened so many years ago."

Ann looked concerned. "Go ahead, I'm listening,"

"Do you remember that time I told you about delivering that box to Aunt Brenda's house and what Uncle Ted said to me that day?"

"Yes?"

"Well, I didn't tell you the whole story. I neglected to tell you that, before I left the place, I picked up a rock from the driveway and threw it through a window."

Ann laughed and said, "I don't think there's a jury in Wood County that would convict you."

Alex laughed too, but then he was beset with coughing spasms. Ann could see that his condition was getting worse and hoped her children would return soon. After her husband's breathing returned to normal, Ann decided to walk down the hallway towards the lounge and make some calls.

CHAPTER   10

Even though Brian couldn't see the peak of the mountain through the trees, he sensed he was near it. The thought of reaching the summit inspired him and because he resisted the temptation of the white horse, adrenaline flowed in his veins. However, the effect was short lived because he now was above the tree line and suffered from lack of oxygen. Going up the mountain, the dirt road had been reduced to a narrow trail with some roots and rocks. When Brian finally reached the ridge, the path turned very rocky and slippery which caused him to fall at times. Even though he ran slower and was more careful, his feet would slide out from under him causing skinned knees and elbows. When he fell the third time, Samuel appeared. Brian gave the angel a wry smile, stood up and began to run with blood dripping from his body. There wasn't room to run together, so Samuel dropped in behind Brian. "You passed a huge test back there, Brian. They sent in the big guns to tempt you, but you prevailed. Keep it up."

Between breaths Brian said, "I'm so tired… I don't know… how much… I have left."

The angel didn't respond. When Brian looked back, he saw for the first time that Samuel had wings. Then the angel rose up above him and flew past until he was out of sight.

As Alex lay there wondering if he was going to die alone, the priest walked into the room. The sight of the clergyman lifted Alex's spirit. "Holy cow Sam, she didn't tell me that you were the new priest."

"I know, I just ran into Ann by the lounge and she told me that. She also told me that you might want some private time alone with me."

"She's a funny girl."

"Right, she told me that Father Matt, God rest his soul, heard your confession a few weeks ago, but that was a few weeks ago."

"Sam, this past month I haven't had the energy to sin."

Sam laughed and said, "Maybe that's a good thing, Alex."

"Yeah, but I sure would like the option."

Sam changed the conversation to a more sentimental tone. "I have nothing but good memories of you, Alex. Growing up, you were like an uncle to me."

Hearing the word 'uncle' triggered a bad memory and Alex told numerous family stories to Sam which he had never heard before.

FLASHBACK #5

Alex refused to call him Great Uncle Gene because it was a misnomer. Instead, he called him 'my dad's uncle'. After the death of Helen Toth, her son Gene evicted Brian and Linda and their baby from the house. He later sold the house, squandered the money and died penniless.

Alex had fond memories of Martha. She had taught him about gardening and house maintenance and treated him like a grandson. After Alex had lost both of his parents, Martha had him move into the big house with her. She had sat in the front pew at the picturesque St. Louis church and witnessed the wedding of Ann and Alex. Later that evening at the reception, she had abandoned her walker and danced with the groom. While on their honeymoon, Alex and Ann received a call informing them that Martha had died while tending to her flower gardens. They acquired permission from the authorities having jurisdiction and had Martha's coffin buried on her property across the ravine, next to her son.

Before Ann, Martha was the only family that Alex knew, besides Aunt Brenda and cousin Sam. After hearing Martha's story about her son Samuel, who had died at the age of three, Brenda had named her son in honor of him. Martha had willed all of her property to Alex and he honed his skills restoring all of the vintage homes in McKee's Corners.

Alex cherished the birth of all of his children, but the memory that stood out the most was the first. When Alexander had held his son for the first time, the words came back to him. Barely audible, he had sung the words by Cat Stevens to the song Father and Son. Forgotten until then, his recollection was jarred and his mind had drifted back to his youth when he would pretend to be asleep, as his father carried him to bed singing the same lyrics. When cousin Sam and Alex's children were old enough to work safely, he took them along to his projects to work and learn. His proudest accomplishment was working with them on the restoration of Aunt Brenda's Haskins House.

Asked about his father, Alex replied, "My dad hovered on the fringe of acceptance. Because of his hard work and determination, not to mention his ultimate gift, I had a good life, much better than his."

When Alexander had begun his storytelling with the priest, family members had started to trickle back into the room and now they had all returned.

Eventually, Alex had talked himself out, was struggling to breath and looked terrible. Ann got Father Sam's attention and seriously nodded at him. The priest took his cue and said, "Alex, I think it's time for me to give you Last Rites."

Alex only nodded. Some of the family members moved in closer, others stepped back.

When the sacrament was completed, Alex appeared calm and strangely energetic. The youngest family members tried to push their way into the room to see what was going on, but were held back by their well-meaning parents. Alex noticed the commotion and said, 'Let the children come to me'.

The adults gave room and youngsters with questions surrounded Alex. The first little girl asked him if he was scared. Alex told them a story about when he was in college. After a hard workout, a teammate of his had asked him if he ever worried about dying. Alex had told him that everyday was a gift and he tried to enjoy every moment. The teammate had told Alex that that philosophy was reflected in his temperament and personality. It was obvious that his answer was too profound for some of the little ones, so he added, "No, I'm not afraid anymore."

Next, a shy boy said, "Tell us the story about when you won the state championship."

A weary Alexander said, "I've told that one a hundred times. You don't want to hear that again, do you?"

Several of them said, "Yes, we do!"

The old man thought about it as he caught his breath. "I'll tell you kids a story about that day that I have never told anyone."

Everyone listened intently as Alex strained to tell the tale. "From the start, I took off fast and had the lead. I thought about the year before, how my dad would run ahead and take short cuts across the course, to wait for me at every mile marker. There were coaches with stopwatches at the mile mark waiting for the runners behind me. I tried to imagine my dad being there for me, but I never saw him. But, the crazy part is, I saw this guy who watched me run by. He looked familiar and for the next mile I tried to figure out who he was. I pushed it hard to the two-mile mark and I was beginning to feel it. That same man was standing there looking at me, but this time he spoke. He said, "Hang in there." And I did. I was really tired that last mile and I think he knew it, but I gave it my all and I saw the man again at the three mile mark. He was standing right in the middle of the final straightaway. When I went by he said, "Your reward will be great." And then I saw that he had wings. They were grayish-white in color and I could see the wind move them. I had hoped to see him at the finish line to talk with, but I never saw him again."

After Alex had finished his story, his condition declined rapidly. Exhaustion overtook him and his breathing was labored. His six children, Ann and Sam held a vigil around the bed. At one point Father Sam suggested that they all hold hands and say a Hail Mary. With his remaining strength, Alex held out his hands to be included. Soon afterwards, between gasps of air, he said, "It is finished," and his ninety-four year old heart stopped beating.

CHAPTER 11

Just when Brian thought he would collapse from exhaustion, the conditions of the path improved. The trail widened and had a modest downhill angle. But most important was the fact that there were no rocks. As he gradually descended the mountain, the trees returned, as did the flowers, birds and the angel. Samuel ran beside him and Brian looked at him with worried eyes. The angel softly said, "Hang in there, Brian."

"I don't know if I can go much farther. How long have I been running?"

"Time has no value here in Purgatory, but I can tell you in Earth terms that you have been at it for fifty-nine years."

Hearing that, Brian staggered, but deftly recovered and caught up with Samuel and said, "How much more penance do I have to do?"

"Oh, you're done with penance, Brian. Your body died a long time ago, we've just been waiting for your heart to stop. It has."

Brian grabbed Samuel's arm and said, "So, you're telling me that Alex has died?"

"Yes."

Brian's eyes began to water.

"Don't be sad, Brian. Your son's body has died, but Alex is waiting for you with the others."

"Where?"

"Just over that hill up ahead."

Immediately, Brian felt revived and the angel disappeared.

All of the sudden, Brian couldn't run fast enough. He lifted his knees and pumped his arms vigorously charging up and over the hill. On the way down, all fatigue and discomfort abandoned his body. The ground leveled out, but he didn't let up. He was unaware of the escort of angels flying above him because he focused all of his attention on the finish line ahead of him. In the distance he could see an elaborate archway with several people standing near the wide opened double gates. He was close enough now that he could hear the cheers and he began to recognize some faces. The first person that he could identify for certain was his grandmother. She still had her hair up in a bun and wore an apron. He couldn't completely understand the words she was saying to him, but he could hear her Hungarian accent. Off to one side stood Martha McKee and next to her there was a tall priest with a bandage on his head. At the other gate, Brian's mom and dad were holding their arms in the air and jumping up and down. He pushed harder and when Brian realized whom the two people were walking towards him, he sprinted. He didn't let up until he reached them. And there, Linda and Alexander welcomed him with open arms.

AFTERWORD

As it turned out, Paradise was real. The good were rewarded and the bad were not. And in the end, Brian met God.